hard crash

Unreal

#1

hard crash

RYAN HUGHES

POCKET BOOKS
New York   London   Toronto   Sydney   Tokyo   Singapore

This book is a work of fiction. Names, characters, places and incidents are products of the author's imagination or are used fictitiously. Any resemblance to actual events or locales or persons living or dead is entirely coincidental.

An *Original* Publication of POCKET BOOKS

POCKET BOOKS, a division of Simon & Schuster Inc.
1230 Avenue of the Americas, New York, NY 10020

Unreal™ ©1997 Epic Megagames, Inc. All rights Reserved. Created by Epic Megagames, Inc. in collaboration with Digital Extremes. Published and distributed by GT Interactive Software Corp. GT is a trademark and the GT logo is a registered trademark of GT Interactive Software Corp. All trademarks are the property of the respective companies.

ISBN: 0-671-01881-7

First Pocket Books printing April 1998

10 9 8 7 6 5 4 3 2 1

POCKET and colophon are registered trademarks of Simon & Schuster Inc.

Printed in the U.S.A.

For Ray Oltion,
in celebration of the freedom
to do what we please

hard crash

Chapter 1

First Occupation

Five months after he found the cave and the voice, Haute, the man who would be known as Prophet, hugged the ground, forcing himself to stay low against the dry grass of the ridgeline. Before him a small valley spread out, peaceful in the hot afternoon sun. But it would soon be far from peaceful. He could feel his heart pounding, and every shallow breath sounded far too loud in his ears. Sweat dripped slowly down the side of his face, and he wished for a wind to help cool him down just a little.

Around him the forest was deadly still, except for a distant low rumbling that seemed to echo off the forest and rock mountains like thunder during a bad storm. Only there were no clouds in the clear sky on this hot day. The rumbling was no natural sound, even though it had become a familiar one to Haute. This sound sent terror through any Nali hearing it, and Haute was no exception.

It was the rumbling of a Skaarj ground transport, headed toward him.

Only this time Haute wasn't running into the trees to hide, afraid to even watch it go past. This time was different, and the pounding of his heart warned him of that very fact.

The rumbling grew slowly louder, and then suddenly the pitch changed completely. Over the far ridge the transport appeared, a cloud of dust billowing out behind it like it was a herd of beasts stampeding.

From what Haute could tell from his distance, there were two Skaarj in the transport. One driving and one riding in the open back, sitting above a dozen Nali prisoners.

Over the last few months, the Skaarj had been rounding up the Nali that had escaped from the castles and hauling them to three major mines. There, the Skaarj were putting them to work as slave labor to mine and stockpile tarydium. From what Haute had heard, the prisoners were fed little, and beaten often. He also had no idea why the Skaarj were stockpiling tarydium, since they had no way of taking it back into space. But maybe they expected a way to come someday.

The transport bounced slowly along the rough road that had only carried wagons and foot traffic before, disappearing and then reappearing from behind stands of trees.

Haute glanced around. Behind him, scattered through the trees, were twenty Nali Mountain Fighters, as they had come to start calling themselves. Most held only long clubs with knives sticking out the sides—the same type of weapon Haute had seen kill a Skaarj in his vision months before.

But two of the men carried Skaarj rifles, just like the one Haute had on the ground beside him. Around his neck he had slung a belt of recharges taken from the dead Skaarj who had once owned the weapon. Each recharge was enough for twenty shots of a high intensity blue and green beam that sliced through almost anything it hit. Haute had used one entire recharge to practice with the rifle, making sure that he could hit what he aimed at.

He slid backward on the ground as the transport disappeared behind a small group of trees. Then he climbed to his feet and ran to his position, ready for the attack.

Just at the top of a fairly steep rise, they had dropped a small tree across the road. Not big enough to make the transport stop, but big enough to slow it down to a crawl as it went over it.

Slow enough for the three of them that carried rifles to get decent shots at the driver and guard.

Haute made sure that he was well hidden, then glanced around at the others. Most he couldn't see, but he knew they were there. With a little luck, in very short order, they would have a transport full of new recruits to help in the fight. Recruits who had been far, far too close to the Skaarj prisons.

The rumbling of the transport filled the air between the trees around them, seeming to shake the leaves and needles. Haute forced himself to take a deep breath. In the five months since he'd warned his home castle about the Skaarj, this was the first real attack they had staged. They had managed to kill three Skaarj and take their weapons, but they had never planned an ambush.

Around the corner, the transport turned into sight. One massive Skaarj frame filled the front, his gaze directed forward as he bounced the transport slowly over the rough road. Haute eased back another inch into his hiding place in the brush as the eyes of the Skaarj driving seemed to bore right into him.

"No panic," he said softly to himself. "Everyone just stay calm."

No one could hear his whispered instruction over the loud roaring of the coming transport, but Haute hoped the others were repeating the same words to themselves. Over the last five months, it had become very clear that the Nali in general were not a fighting people. They didn't know how, and when faced with fighting, their natural reaction was to turn and run, or just cower.

Haute knew he could fight. He had proven that to himself when he and Targee and three others had killed the first Skaarj. And the other two with Skaarj rifles on this mission had proven they could stand and fight, also.

It was the others, crouching in the brush with only knives and clubs, that were along for the experience more than for actually fighting. Haute hoped they would never even have the chance to move, let alone fight with those clubs. But they needed to see what fighting and death was really like, and if they could, then do it. Haute expected at least half of them would not be able to.

The transport slowed as it approached the fallen tree, the rumbling so loud Haute couldn't imagine riding in the back of the open transport. The front wheels of the transport were now almost even with his position.

He could smell the rancid smell from the engine and feel the faint headache he always got when near tarydium. If this worked as he had planned, he

4

wouldn't be near the tarydium long enough for his headache to even get bad.

"No panic," he said. "Just do it."

The front wheels were now past him.

"Timing," he said softly to himself. "Wait."

"Wait."

The front wheels touched the fallen tree. Haute took a deep breath.

The front wheels eased over the tree.

Haute stood.

The front wheels hit the ground on the other side of the tree.

Haute swung the rifle up, aimed it at the side of the head of the Skaarj driver, and fired.

The strange weapon pulsed in his hands, a blue and green beam of energy shooting out.

The driver's head vanished in a spray of blood, skin, and bones, coating the green brush on the other side of the road with the red and white remains.

Haute's heart seemed to freeze in his chest. He had accomplished his part of the mission. He had killed the driver.

And for an instant, he stared at the headless body and the blood splattered beyond it.

Then the instant ended.

The Skaarj guard standing above the Nali prisoners seemed stunned at the sudden fire coming from the brush. He turned and saw Haute, his black eyes seeming to cut through to Haute's very soul.

Haute swung his gun toward the guard.

The guard started to raise his weapon to fire at Haute.

Then suddenly the guard went over backward as two other beams from Skaarj weapons cut out through the trees.

Both beams caught the Skaarj guard squarely in the chest, smashing him up and out of the transport like a leaf before a sudden burst of wind.

Targee and Bccui had both accomplished their mission: they had killed the guard.

The transport jerked to a stop, front wheels on one side of the fallen tree, back wheels on the other. With a quick sputter, the roaring stopped.

Suddenly around Haute, the silence of the forest rushed back in, seemingly almost as loud as the transport.

No birds chirped.

No wind rustled the trees.

Nothing but silence.

Haute sprang from the brush and moved quickly around the front of the transport, rifle at the ready just in case. But, as he knew would be the case, the Skaarj guard was dead, his insides completely vaporized by the two shots.

"All clear!" Haute shouted into the silence.

Suddenly a wild cheer went up from all around the transport, echoing through the trees and over the valley below. Seemingly out of everywhere, Haute's Mountain Fighters stood and came forward from their hiding positions. Haute was sure that many of them were cheering at the relief of not having to fight. But at the moment that didn't matter.

They had won!

They had killed two Skaarj, captured their weapons and a transport.

Haute moved around to the back of the large, black vehicle as the others gathered around the crowd of prisoners in the back, all cheering and talking at once. But it was clear to Haute that the prisoners were almost as confused and afraid as before. They were cowering in the back, as if waiting to be killed.

And who could blame them. The guard that had been standing above them had been blown clear out of the transport. They would have no way of knowing that they wouldn't be next.

"Quiet!" Haute shouted, then he shoved his way to the edge of the transport. He climbed up near the prisoners, as his men quieted down.

"Targee," Haute said to his friend from the first night at the lake, "get the Skaarj rifles and ammunition belts. Bccui, you and two others help him."

Targee and Bccui both nodded and turned away. Two others instantly split off from the men, moving toward the dead guard in the brush first. Haute noticed which two and committed their faces to memory. They would be fighters. They wanted weapons. That, for a Nali, was a very good sign.

Haute then turned to the prisoners. They had clearly come from a number of different castles, and from the looks of them, had lived a hard five months since the crash of the Skaarj ship. Most of their clothes were filthy and torn. All of them were coated with dust from the trip. It was clear that many of them needed water almost immediately.

"Don't worry," Haute said to the shocked and dirty faces staring at him. "You've been rescued by the Nali Mountain Fighters. My name is Haute. You are free to go your own way, or come with us to help fight the Skaarj. The choice is yours."

A uniform look of shock and questions filled the prisoners' eyes.

Haute felt bad for them, but now was not the time to ease their worries. "Right now, I need you to get out of the transport as quickly as possible and move a short distance down the road."

Haute turned to the rest of his men standing around the transport, smiling. "Everyone help someone out and down the road toward the stream. They all need water and food."

Instantly, numbers of Haute's men started to climb on the transport. Haute jumped down and went around to the front of the truck, where Targee was digging the driver's weapon out from under the body.

"This went well," Haute said. "As good as I had hoped."

"It will not always be easy," Targee said, his voice low and flat.

Haute knew that Targee was a man of few words. But when he did say something, it was usually right. And in this case, Haute knew he was very, very right. From the scouting they had managed to do in the first five months, they knew there had been more than two hundred Skaarj on the ship that crashed. So far, they had killed five. They had a long way to go before ridding the planet of the monsters from the stars. A very long way.

Targee yanked the ammunition belt off the Skaarj's body, then slung it over his head and across his chest with the other belt. With his broad shoulders, ammunition belts, and a heavy Skaarj weapon in each upper hand, Targee looked more like a fighter than the Skaarj. He would strike fear into any person who didn't know him.

"Sir?" a voice said from behind Haute.

Haute turned to face a young man, not many years into his adulthood. He had been one of the prisoners on the transport, and his face was coated with dirt, some of which had caked into mud around his mouth.

"My name is Haute. What's yours?"

"Rentahs, sir," the young man said.

Haute smiled. "No sir. Just Haute. Now what can I help you with?"

Rentahs nodded, then pointed at the place where the guard had been standing above the prisoners. "I think you need to check, in there."

Haute glanced at the platform, then back at Rentahs. "You want to help me?" Haute asked, climbing up the side of the transport.

Both Targee and Rentahs climbed up beside him, then Haute saw what Rentahs had meant. The platform that the Skaarj guard had been standing on was also a storage area of some sort. There was a small latch, square in the middle.

Haute glanced at Targee, who only shrugged, but pointed one of the rifles at the box just in case.

Haute nodded, then flipped open the latch and lifted.

At first he didn't completely understand what he was looking at.

Then Targee laughed. A short, almost snort sort of laugh.

And for some reason that laugh cleared Haute's mind, and he saw the contents of the storage compartment: weapons.

Dozens of Skaarj beam weapons and boxes of ammunition refills.

Haute glanced first at Targee, who was smiling, then at Rentahs, who was also smiling, cracking the dirt that caked his face.

"Take one," Haute said to Rentahs, pointing at the weapons. "It would seem you deserve one."

Rentahs smile broadened.

"Only one condition," Haute said.

"What's that, sir?"

"Two conditions, actually," Haute said. "You want to fight with us against the Skaarj."

Rentahs nodded quickly. "I will fight."

"Second," Haute said, "you don't call me sir."

Rentahs laughed. "Fighting beside you against those monsters would be an honor." He reached down and picked up a weapon, hefting it like he'd been born with one in his hands.

Haute watched. And for the moment, he felt slightly better about the chances of the Nali winning the long fight. They would stand a chance if they could find more like Rentahs.

Maybe.

Chapter 2

Second Occupation

Melnori's arms ached. Having all four of them tied together in an X across his backpack was an uncomfortable position to begin with, and being forced to walk across rough ground that way was even worse. But he had insisted that his captors let him lead them away from the Skaarj patrols that would certainly come looking for the people who had destroyed the tarydium mine.

They didn't trust him enough to let him free, but they did at least believe him when he told them that they were in danger. That was a start. The Prophet alone knew how things had gotten off to such a bad beginning with these creatures, but getting them to listen to him was a step in the right direction.

He had decided to take them up to Tien Camp, a secluded notch in Sopiny Canyon, where they could rest without fear of discovery. It had been an old tarydium mine centuries ago, one of the few mines the Nali had excavated on their own before the

11

coming of the Skaarj, but it was played out long ago. Now it was a lush green meadow boxed in by a steep forested hillside to the north, cliffs to the east and west, and the river to the south, and it was one of Melnori's favorite places. Difficult to find even for those who knew about it, it had recovered from its ignoble beginnings to become one of the few unspoiled places left on the planet. There, Melnori could take off his clothes and bathe naked in the stream, tickle golden trout out from under rocks and cook them over a campfire for breakfast—live for at least a few days as the Nali had lived before the Skaarj had come from the sky to enslave them.

From Tien Camp, he could also send a message down the river to let the resistance know what he had found, and tell them that he still hadn't infiltrated Rrajigar as planned. That wasn't really a setback so much as a delay; he wasn't the only agent attempting to penetrate the Skaarj stronghold, and while attacking it had been an outside possibility deemed worthy of investigation, nobody seriously thought it could succeed.

Now, Melnori wondered. Aliens always added a new factor to every equation. The human light gun—a laser, Zofia had called it—was something new, and while it wouldn't affect the outcome of a planetwide war, it might decide a battle somewhere. And wars were won battle by battle. If they could get enough factors to work in their favor, maybe the Nali *could* march on Rrajigar. And from there they could retake the stronghold at Bluff Eversmoking, and then on to the Loche of the Underflow, and so on around the planet.

It was a grand dream. Perhaps an impossible one, but dreams had kept the Nali going for centuries when nothing else could. Dreams of a time when peace would return to Na Pali, when people of all different races could live together in harmony and create a beautiful future together.

He wondered if the humans had such dreams. Most races did. Some even codified them into religions.

He remembered the wooden box he had found on board the human starship, the one with the carved image of a man in agony on the cover. Tied to a cross of wood in much the same fashion as Melnori was tied to himself, in fact. That and the obviously ceremonial nature of the contents had practically shouted "religion!" at him, but it was hard to imagine how such a horrible image could represent a philosophy of peace and hope.

Especially after he had seen how these humans reacted to danger. Blowing up an entire mine just to create a diversion! No Nali would ever have considered that. No Nali would even have *thought* of it in the first place.

That was another new factor in the equation. The humans thought differently. They might come up with solutions to the problem that the Nali had overlooked. Some of them might be horrible, but some might not.

And perhaps the humans could be guided in the right direction, taught to think in ways more useful to the Nali. Maybe if they were presented with a new set of ideals, they could be persuaded to adopt them as their own. The religious impulse was obviously there. Maybe these creatures simply needed a better example.

It would be a dangerous undertaking. Their differences were the most valuable part of their makeup; if he succeeded too well he could destroy that. But these were dangerous times. If he didn't try something, he could lose a unique opportunity. And it wasn't like they were much use now. As it was, these humans were fixated completely on their own concerns. If he could expand their perspective a little, get them to consider the bigger picture, they would be far more likely to help the Nali.

They were drawing close to the slope that led down into Tien Camp. Melnori turned to the three humans, Zofia and Boris supporting Gerick's weight as they walked, and said, "We are nearly to safety."

"Good," said Zofia. "I'm getting tired of carrying this slacker."

Gerick exhaled loudly. "Ha! If you were carrying me, I wouldn't hurt so much."

Melnori showed his teeth, as he had watched the humans do when they were amused. "You should look at this situation as a chance for all of you to improve your *sha*. Zofia and Boris gain *sha* by demonstrating their willingness to sacrifice their comfort for another. Gerick gains *sha* by providing the opportunity for compassion."

"That's a laugh," said Zofia. "Gerick having anything to do with compassion."

Boris said, "Sounds like karma. We discredited that system mathematically a couple of centuries back. It led to infinities, division by zero—all sorts of contradictions."

"Did it? Interesting." Melnori smiled again, undeterred. At least they were familiar with the concept. "We are not concerned with the accounting so much as the result. The opportunity to better oneself, to make the best of whatever situation life presents to us." He spoke these words to Zofia. She seemed to be the leader of these three, even though Gerick thought he was. Melnori could see who really held the power here.

"That's different from karma," she said. "Everybody wants to make something of themselves. Even Gerick, right?"

He winced as he put his weight on the wrong foot. "I want to make a nice big bed and lie down in it for a week. Preferably under a quarter gee or less. Spiritual enlightenment can wait until I'm rested."

Melnori slipped on a rock and nearly fell, but Boris reached out and steadied him. "Thank you," said Melnori. "Your *sha* has increased. So has mine."

"No, it was purely selfish on my part," Boris said. "If you hurt yourself, we'll have to carry you, too."

Melnori knew he was joking, but the joke itself betrayed how alien his thoughts were. "Why do you deny the more noble motive?" he asked, truly puzzled.

None of the humans answered.

"That was a serious inquiry," Melnori said. "I am trying to understand your thought processes."

Zofia said, "All right, then. He denied it because it wouldn't be as noble if he admitted it. It would make him a sanctimonious bastard instead."

She had used a non-Vrenic word. "Define that, please."

"Hypocritical. Claiming to be more holy than he really is. It's like macho. If you go around telling people how tough you are, you're not as tough as if you keep it to yourself and just live that way."

Another alien concept. Melnori was racking them up right and left. "So, a human can't admit to being either tough or nice," he said.

"Pretty much. Some people do, but the rest of us usually make fun of them behind their backs."

Gerick laughed. "Of course, some of us are so cosmically tough that we can tell everybody we're the toughest goddamned bastards they'll ever meet and still have enough left over to make up the difference."

"Theoretically speaking, of course," said Zofia. "Ow!"

Gerick had stepped on her foot.

"Then there're the ones that're just obstinate," she said, punching him in the ribs with her free hand. He had one of his arms over her shoulder and one over Boris's, so he couldn't hit back. A decided disadvantage to having only two, thought Melnori.

He was beginning to get a picture of these people, though. Basically well-intentioned, but culturally unable to express it. Yearning for fulfillment, but unable to admit it. What a tangled mess these humans were. No wonder their god—if that's what the image on the wooden box was—looked like he was in pain. The weight of these pitiful people's tormented souls must crush anyone who truly cared about them.

Fortunately, Melnori didn't have that problem. He supposed his *sha* would suffer from the admission, but he had enough concerns trying to free the Nali.

He had learned enough. It was time to make use of his knowledge.

"The Skaarj seem to share much of your philosophy," he said. "They never admit to compassion, they use strength for personal gain, and they despise the weak."

"That's . . . uh . . . that's a pretty harsh comparison," said Zofia. "From what I've seen, the Skaarj are outright bastards even by human standards."

"Perhaps, but all the same, I am disappointed."

Gerick made a rude snorting noise with his lips.

"Aww, that's too bad. We were hoping so much to impress you with how *nice* we were."

Melnori shook his head from side to side, another gesture he had learned by watching the humans. "Nice is not required. Purity of heart is. You see, there is a prophecy that dates back centuries ago, back to the days when the Skaarj first tried to enslave us. Our greatest prophet predicted that they would eventually succeed, but he also had a vision. He saw an avenging angel come down out of the heavens to help us defeat the Skaarj. For a moment I had thought one of you might be that angel, but given your philosophy, that is obviously not the case."

"Obviously," said Gerick.

Neither Zofia nor Boris said anything.

The slope they were descending was steep, but Melnori could see it level off not far below, and a patch of brightness shone golden through the trees. "We are nearly there," he said.

Chapter 3

First Occupation

Haute couldn't believe their luck. Not only had they killed two Skaarj, but it turned out there were twelve weapons and thirty boxes of ammunition in the storage area in the transport.

After giving one Skaarj weapon to young Rentahs, who had pointed out the guns, Haute and Targee quickly handed the weapons down off the transport and had them stacked twenty paces down the road. Haute would have to get a few others to help them carry the guns back to the caverns. That was a great problem and one he had never counted on having. With the weapons the dead Skaarj had carried, they had fourteen new weapons.

Fourteen Skaarj weapons to kill Skaarj. Their first mission had been a complete success, so far.

"Okay," Haute said. "Let's take anything we might need off this as fast as we can. Targee, you and Bccui start at the front. Rentahs and I will work through this end."

Haute took a deep breath and forced the headache to stay back. The two dead Skaarj were full of tarydium, in their suits and their very bodies. He could not only feel it, but smell it. And the truck was powered by a form of tarydium. Haute's sensitivity to tarydium was starting to kick in, from just being close to these small amounts of it. He'd have to be away from here in fifteen minutes, or someone might have to carry him.

Haute could also tell that Targee was having the same problem of sensitivity. Only when he got near tarydium, he started to break out. His face was already red and blotchy, and in another hour he'd be covered in welts and blisters.

After ten minutes, they had pulled off lights, wiring, and a device that looked like a form of battery that wasn't tarydium-powered. They had also found a dozen other items. Haute had no idea what they might be, but someone thought each item might come in handy in the future, so they took it.

Haute also found a small bottle of what looked to be a form of medicine, stashed under the seat. He'd never seen anything like it before, but he took it anyhow, figuring that someone back at the cave might figure out what it was for. They had more than enough help doing that sort of thing. It was fighters who could kill Skaarj that they were short of.

After the transport had been gone over completely, Haute had everyone move back down the road near the weapons pile. Just being twenty paces from the tarydium eased the headache. He was glad this was almost over.

He turned to Targee. "Ready?"

Targee nodded.

They had decided the night before, back in the cave, that if they managed to stop and capture a transport, they wouldn't try to keep it. They had no place to hide it, and why take the chance of the Skaarj recapturing it and using it again. Instead, they had decided to destroy it, a decision that Haute had very much wanted. And now that he was standing here, weapon in hand, headache throbbing, he knew it was the right decision.

"Fire," Haute said.

Beams of intense blue light flashed out from their rifles and hit the truck. Haute could feel the Skaarj rifle pulsing in his hand, and it made him feel secure. Almost powerful.

The beams cut into the frame of the truck, exploding parts in all directions.

Smoke rose into the air as they continued to cut back and forth through the transport, vaporizing parts, shearing other parts off.

Finally Targee said, "Enough."

Haute clicked his weapon off just a short moment before the charge was about to expire. The transport was now nothing more than a large mound of smoking metal, clogging the middle of the road like a giant, misshapen rock. It would take someone a long time to even identify it as a transport. It would never, ever be used to haul Nali prisoners again. Haute had no doubt even that the road was going to have to find a new path around it.

Haute stared at the very clear signal they were leaving for the Skaarj, memorizing its very shape. The resistance had started.

And now the Skaarj would know it. They were leaving a very clear sign.

For some reason, Haute doubted the Skaarj would even be worried.

He turned to Targee and the young, dirt-covered Rentahs. "Let's go home."

"And where's home?" Rentahs asked.

"You will soon see," he said.

"And we have baths, also," Targee said, patting the young Nali on the back before starting to pick up some of the items salvaged from the transport.

Rentahs laughed nervously, glancing down at his filthy clothes and dirt-caked arms. "Thank the gods."

Haute laughed. "You might *not* say that when you feel the temperature of the water."

Six long hours later, with less than an hour of sunlight left in the sky, they finally led those who wanted to join them to the cave, bringing along the weapons and salvaged parts of the transport.

Since the decision, five months before, to use the series of caverns for headquarters and shelter, the place had grown almost comfortable. And to Haute, right at that moment, after a long day, it felt great to be home.

He assigned each new resident a current cave occupant to explain all the rules and safety precautions, and give a tour. Then he told each new resident to get cleaned up, get food, and then report to Jeeie in the main cavern for duty assignment.

He told the young Rentahs to stay at his side for the moment, and he'd give him the tour. There was just something about the young Nali that Haute liked. Maybe it was the anger in his eyes. Haute didn't know, yet. But he wanted to find out. And the only way was to keep the kid close for a short time.

Ablee greeted his old friend just inside the mouth of the cave, smiling. Ablee had completely taken over the duties of cooking for the hundred who lived in the caverns now.

Jeeie was the duty master, sending out hunting parties for food, scheduling guards for all entrances into and out of the valley, and otherwise running the daily duties of such a growing community. He was also in charge of a vast spy network, bringing in more and more information about Skaarj movements and habits.

Haute's brother Bccui had become a leader of a second strike force, just as Haute and Targee were. It seemed that both he and his brother had a knack for fighting Skaarj. Bccui's other main job was to train a new crew of fighters, both in weapons' fire and in how to kill a Skaarj with nothing more than a knife or a club.

"Successful mission, Prophet?" Ablee asked Haute, then glanced at Rentahs. Rentahs didn't notice, since he was staring, openmouthed at the beauty of the huge cavern. Twenty torches lit the space as if it were daylight. And at least fifty Nali were in the main room at the moment, some working, some just moving from one place to another.

"More than we could have imagined," Haute said, slapping his old friend, Ablee, on the back. "Let me tell everyone at the same time."

Haute stepped past Ablee and toward the center of the large main cavern. As he did, he was greeted with questions from those who were working or milling around the huge area. He held each question off with a quick, "I'll tell everyone."

Haute climbed up on the huge rock in the center of

the cavern, and held his arms up for attention and silence. When everyone in the cave was looking up at him, he smiled, glancing around at all the people who had come to follow him.

"I have good news. We were completely successful in stopping the transport and rescuing at least twenty who were headed for slave labor in the mines."

A huge cheer filled the cavern, echoing back and forth so loudly that Haute wondered if it might knock stones down from the ceiling. He let the cheer go on for a short moment, then held up his hands again. Quickly, the room calmed down to silence.

"We killed two Skaarj, destroyed their transport, and captured fourteen new weapons with ammunition."

At the news about the weapons, the cheering resumed, this time even louder, as Haute climbed down, smiling. Many, many in this room were not capable of fighting Skaarj. But everyone here knew how important what they were doing was. And how important the new weapons were to all their safety.

With a large number of congratulations and pats on the back, Haute moved back over to Ablee and Rentahs.

"Add about fifteen to the dinner count tonight," Haute said to Ablee. "Almost all the rescued ones came with us."

"I'm going to need more help in the kitchen," Ablee said, shaking his head. "And Jeeie will need to send out more fishing and hunting parties."

"You'll manage," Haute said, laughing. "We have so far. Just don't pick anyone who wants to fight."

Ablee glanced at young Rentahs.

Rentahs pressed his hand on the ammunition belt

he had slung over his shoulder and across his chest. "I'd like to fight," he said, glancing at Ablee, then back to Haute. "If it's all right with you?"

"It's great with me," Haute said, and the boy beamed through the dirt on his face.

Ablee laughed. "Go out and risk your life to get out of kitchen duty. Now I've heard it all." With another loud laugh, he turned and headed across the cavern toward the tunnel that went back into the kitchen area.

"Don't mind him," Haute said, smiling at Rentahs. "Ablee's the best cook in the world. Come on, let's get you cleaned up and find you some clean clothes. Then I'll give you a tour of your new home."

Three hours later, after a great dinner of meat stew and fresh-baked bread, Haute and the rest of the main Mountain Fighters council sat around a small fire in a cavern just off the kitchen.

The council, as just about everyone living in the cave called it, had sort of formed from the first nights around the fire, planning. It seemed that every night, after dinner, the group met and worked on the next day's duties and needs. And then, as more and more joined the fighters, the council became a distinct governing body.

It consisted of Haute, Targee, Bccui, Ablee, and Jeeie. They had set aside the small cave off the kitchen area to use for a meeting room every evening, which became known as the council chamber. Of course, it also stored baskets of roots, barrels full of torch oil, and other supplies. But since the five of them met there every night, it was called the council room.

Tonight the mood of all five was festive, because of the success of the transport mission earlier. But Haute had gotten past most of his celebration. During most of the hike back to the cave, he had worried about what to do next. And for the life of him, he couldn't come up with anything more than a nagging feeling that he was overlooking something.

After everyone had settled down on his own stump or rock, Haute started the meeting with his worry. "Okay, what next?"

Ablee shrugged. "We do what we have planned. We go after more and more Skaarj, killing one at a time, until they're all gone from the planet."

Bccui nodded. "Agreed. Especially now that we have more weapons."

The others all nodded, but Ablee was staring at Haute with a puzzled frown on his face. "It seems," Ablee said, "that our prophet doesn't agree completely. Am I right, my friend?"

Haute shook his head. "You know, I honestly don't know."

And he didn't. One part of his mind just said there was something very important missing. But he couldn't put his finger on what it might be.

Ablee nodded. "Then let's go over the plan again. See if we can spot where something is going wrong."

"I'm not sure that it is," Haute said.

"I've been around you long enough to trust those feelings of yours," Ablee said. "We go over the plan again."

Haute nodded, and Ablee started, outlining slowly what the group had planned in its methods of splitting into teams of between ten and twenty, attacking single Skaarj where they could find them, transports if they could. And for at least the next few months, they were going to stay away from the castles. Instead, they would stay in the mountains, keep on looking for more weapons and recruiting more Nali to their cause.

Ablee finished, with everyone nodding in agreement. Even Haute knew the plan was solid. But he still felt as if something was missing.

He sat back and stared up at the orange light from the fire, dancing along the rocks and crevices of the ceiling. Suddenly, the image of his own death flashed through his mind again. He could almost feel the pain of the thorns and the pounding in his head of the tarydium reaction.

And with that image, he knew what he had to do.

He stared at Ablee, then smiled slowly.

"I think he's figured it out," Ablee said, laughing.

"So tell us," Jeeie said.

"I still haven't figured out what I'm missing," Haute said. "But I know where I can find the answer."

For a moment Ablee stared at him with a puzzled expression, then slowly he realized what Haute was talking about. And as he did, a look of worry came over his face.

Haute had to make a pilgrimage.

He had to go back to the mountain, to another cave, and to a voice that had once led him through a vision of his own coming death. It was the only way to find out where they were heading.

And if that direction was the right one.

Chapter 4

Second Occupation

Zofia felt the sting in Melnori's words. As she helped set up camp—making a real lean-to shelter now, and refilling her water bottle in the river—she couldn't help but think about what he had said. Not pure enough to be the Nali messiah, eh? That was certainly true enough, given her past, but did it have to be so obvious?

Just once in her life she would like to feel needed. Not the way she had been needed in the break-in at the starship works—for her code-breaking skill and her invincible attitude—nor even the way she was needed here to help carry Gerick away from the Skaarj. She would like to be needed for something more important than that, something more personal. For her character.

That was a laugh. Melnori may not have been the soul of tact, but he had pegged her right. She had never met a situation she couldn't screw up, never helped someone out without expecting something in return, never—

Wait a minute, she thought. When the *Vortex Rikers* had crashed, who had immediately started helping other people out of their cells? When the Skaarj had come, who had stuck around to protect those same people? Granted, she hadn't laid down her life for the others the way Jack or the Australian guy had, but she was pretty damned proud of what she *had* done. All without a single thought for herself.

Well, okay, maybe she was hoping that somebody among the prisoners could help her get free, but still, it wasn't like she was charging them by the hour or anything.

An avenging angel, eh? Why the hell couldn't she be the one? Not that she believed in some silly alien prophecy for a second, but just for the sake of argument, why not? She wondered if wanting something like that to be true was akin to saying you were macho. If you want to be the messiah, you're not qualified.

Hah. The New Washington colony had tried that approach with their leaders, voting into office the people who least wanted the job, and they had wound up with the worst idiots in the galaxy. After their economic collapse, they had immediately installed a fascist dictator and were glad to have him. All of humanity had learned from that debacle: if you want something done right, hire someone who wants to do it.

That let her off the hook. Zofia had no more desire to become an alien avatar than she had to become a fascist dictator. All she really wanted was to get off this damned planet—preferably without going back to prison—and try a fresh start somewhere else. Of course, if Melnori was telling the truth about the situation here, she might just have to help him drive the Skaarj off the planet first, but she didn't have to fulfill some silly prophecy to do that. Sacking a city or two and stealing a starship ought to be sufficient.

As she walked back into their camp with her water bottle dripping cold river water, she caught Boris looking off into the distance, lost in thought.

"Boris Liang, avenging angel?" she asked softly. "Has quite a ring to it, doesn't it?"

He jerked back to the present, blushing guiltily. "I—I wasn't—"

"Sure, you weren't. Come on, hero, let's see if we can get a campfire going. It's going to be a cold night without sleeping bags."

She was right about that. Melnori wouldn't allow more than a tiny fire, and even that had to be hidden, down at the bottom of a foot-high circle of rocks, and overshadowed by the densest tree near their campsite. "The Skaarj can see heat emissions," he said. "If we light a big fire, we might as well just walk into Rrajigar and turn ourselves in."

Zofia had seen the wisdom in that. So she and Boris and Gerick had put on all their clothing and huddled near the tiny flickering flames, warming their hands on the rocks when the fire's heat finally soaked through them. When they could no longer stay awake, they lay down beside the fire and curled up together. Zofia got the middle, since neither Boris nor Gerick would snuggle with the other even if the alternative was to freeze to death. She was the warmest of the three, but only because of their intolerance of each other.

As she drifted off to sleep, she wondered how that affected her *sha*.

Melnori didn't need to snuggle, nor did he sleep, so far as she could tell. When Zofia woke up in the night, she saw him still sitting there by the fire, his back to the tree trunk where they had tied him for the night, wrapped in a cloak from his pack.

Overhead, a shooting star burned across the sky. A *big* shooting star. Zofia saw tongues of flame burst from it, and a few seconds after it disappeared over the horizon she saw a bright flash. A few minutes later the ground rumbled a little.

"Another starship?" she whispered.

Melnori's eyes glittered in the starry night. "Perhaps it's an avenging angel," he said.

She didn't dignify that with an answer.

The next time she awoke, dawn was breaking. The eastern sky looked like it was on fire, and the trees and rocks in the canyon glowed with a golden light. Zofia sat up, stiff and cold, but she was smiling. Despite the discomfort, there were definitely pluses to camping out.

They stayed at Tien Camp for three days, ostensibly waiting for the regeneration drugs from their medkits to repair Gerick's broken ankle, but everyone knew the real reason. They had found a pocket of calm in the midst of chaos, and nobody wanted to give it up. Not even Melnori, who spent the first two days with his hands tied together. Zofia felt a bit sorry for him, but whenever she started to weaken, she would remember the way he had fired the laser at her. Maybe he could be trusted, but she wasn't going to bet her life on it anytime soon.

The matter was decided for her on the third morning, when she woke to a wonderful aroma and found him humming softly while he cooked four bright

yellow fish over the campfire. He had shoved forked
sticks into their backs so he could hold them out
horizontally over the flames, and they were sizzling
nicely as he tended them, one stick in each of his
untied hands.

"Good morning," he said when he saw that she was
awake.

"How did you get free?" she asked.

He made a complicated little shrug of his shoulders
that didn't move the fish. "Magic," he said.

"Yeah, right."

"I needed a bath," he said. "I was beginning to
stink, which is a very unpleasant sensation for a
Nali." The way he said it implied that it wasn't
necessarily a problem for a human. Zofia vowed to
take a dip in the river herself, even though the water
was cold enough to freeze a frog.

"So now that you're free, you expect us to just let
you stay that way?" she asked.

"Yes," he said. "You see, I sent a message this
morning to the leader of the resistance. Assuming the
message makes it to the pickup point by noon, she
should arrive sometime before dark to talk with you.
It would probably make a poor impression if she
found me tied up."

Zofia sat up and rubbed the sleep from her eyes.
"On the other hand, it might let her know we mean
business."

"It might. Or it might confirm your cruelty. It's
your choice. I'll be free again soon enough after she
arrives."

"And maybe we'll be gone," Zofia said. "We didn't
agree to meet anybody."

"Gerick's leg is nowhere near ready to walk on yet,

31

and you know it. In fact, that is why I called for help today. Your regeneration drugs are taking far too long to heal him. It's time we took him to our stronghold and did it properly."

Gerick had evidently been listening. He opened his eyes at the sound of his name. "I'm not taking any alien drugs," he said.

"No one is asking you to," said Melnori. "We can heal you in an hour without risk."

"How do you know that? I thought humans were new to you."

Melnori turned the fish over. "Our methods heal anyone from any race."

Zofia felt herself grow interested despite her skepticism. Her cracked rib still bothered her when she moved wrong. She could imagine how Gerick must feel with a broken ankle. He was hobbling around on a crutch they had cut from a forked branch, but Melnori was right; he was a long way from healed.

Boris woke up at that point, and Zofia explained to him what Melnori had told her and Gerick, but when Boris pressed him for evidence he could believe, the Nali refused to elaborate.

"You either trust us, or you don't," he said. "It's your choice."

"No," said Zofia. "We'll take it one step at a time. We'll leave you untied, but under guard. We'll talk to this leader of yours when she shows up. We may even go with you to where you can heal Gerick's leg, if you can convince us it's possible."

"Maybe?" asked Gerick. "Speak for yourself, twitch."

"Maybe I'll let you go alone, and see if you come back in one piece," she said to him.

That gave him something to think about. She didn't

wait around for a reply; she left him and Boris to guard Melnori while she got up and walked through the trees to the stream bank, checking her automag, tarydium gun, and her flak gun as she went, to make sure Melnori hadn't fooled with them while she slept. Apparently he hadn't; they looked ready to go.

The water was just as cold as she remembered it. Zofia stripped down and stuck her feet in it anyway, and splashed as much on herself and rubbed as much as she could stand. Maybe she could freeze off the sweat and the dirt.

She felt considerably better after she'd dressed and warmed up again, and by the time she got back to the camp, Melnori had finished cooking the fish. They tasted odd—more like chewy grapes than like fish flesh—but they were fresh food and they revived her spirits just as much as the bath had.

Knowing somebody was coming today heightened her awareness, too. Zofia felt more awake, more alert, than she had since the crash. Every sense seemed to have opened up today; she could smell the separate aromas of leaves and flowers and warm ground, feel the breeze tickle the tiny hairs on her forearms and neck, hear the subliminal rumble of rocks shifting in the riverbed. She felt almost supernatural, an elemental creature of the forest.

So she had a moment's warning when the Skaarj flyer banked around the downstream cliffs and advanced on the camp.

She was sunning herself on a rock by the water. The moment the gray, bullet-shaped vehicle hove into view, something told her it didn't carry the individual she was waiting for. Just based on what she knew of Melnori, she thought its bulbous cockpit and stubby landing legs looked too utilitarian for the Nali to have built it, and the oversized gun ports on either side looked much too sinister.

Without even thinking about it, she drew both her flak gun and the tarydium gun—the stinger, Melnori had called it—and rolled over the edge of the rock into the water. The chill hit her like an electric shock, but she didn't scream, and she didn't let either gun get wet. She didn't worry about the automag; it could soak for weeks and still fire. She let the current push her up against the rock, hiding her from view, and she waited until the flyer slipped overhead.

She raised the stinger, looking for a vulnerable spot. The flyer wasn't particularly large—seven or eight feet wide and twice that long, but the entire underside was armored against attack from below.

The pilot saw the camp site and veered toward it. The flyer rolled sideways with the sudden motion, then righted itself.

It was only ten feet or so off the water; when it approached the bank, it was only six or eight feet above the rocks. Zofia didn't know why, not on a conscious level, but just as it swept past, she set her stinger on the rock and lunged out of the water, pulled herself up onto the bank, and leaped for the hindmost landing leg, wrapping her left arm around the strut and letting her weight yank it downward.

That was the wrong arm to be grabbing with. Her cracked rib gave her a jolt that made her gasp, but she managed to hang on. The back of the flyer dipped, its vectored force beams momentarily unable to compensate for the extra load. Zofia's butt slammed hard into a rock, then the pilot corrected for the tilt, and the landing leg yanked her into the air again.

That was too much for her. She let go and the flyer

rocked far forward, then tilted crazily back. She transferred the fragger over to her left hand, grabbed onto the landing skid again with her right, and jumped back in the river. This time the flyer tilted almost vertical before it corrected itself. She let it haul her back out of the water before she let go again, and that was enough: the pilot overcompensated and the flyer flipped completely over onto its top, slamming down into the rocky riverbank under full power.

The cockpit shattered into a spray of gravelly shards. Zofia, looking inside from underneath, saw two upside-down Skaarj struggling to crawl from their seats. She aimed her flak gun straight into their astonished faces and fired point-blank, *boom boom,* and they fell limp, their heads gone.

There was nobody else in the flyer. Zofia climbed out of the river and shook the water out of her clothes. She heard shouts from camp and saw Boris and Melnori running toward her, weapons drawn. Gerick was standing by the fire with the laser rifle.

"Are you all right?" Boris shouted when he drew close.

She couldn't stop shivering. "Y-y-yeah, I g-g-guess so."

He crouched down behind a rock and peered into the upside-down flyer, ready to shoot anything that moved, but it was obvious from the blood gushing out of their ragged necks that the two Skaarj weren't going to cause anybody any more trouble. He stood up again and climbed around the flyer to stand beside Zofia.

"How did you do that?" he asked. "I didn't hear any shots until after it crashed."

"I—I t-t-tipped it ov-v-ver," she said. "Unb-b-balanced it. J-j-*jesus* that water's c-c-cold."

Boris put his arms around her to help warm her up, but that just pressed her cold clothing against her skin. She moved gently out of his embrace and said, "Come on, h-help me push this m-m-mother back over. If it s-still works, m-m-maybe we can use it."

"You just tipped it over?" Boris asked. "Just like that?"

Melnori was looking at her with an inscrutable expression on his long face.

"All in a d-d-day's work for the av-v-venging angel," she said, looking him straight in the eye. "C-come on, you, t-t-too," she said, stepping up to the edge of the flyer and grabbing hold. Equally speechless, both Melnori and Boris came up beside her. She wished she could enjoy the moment more, but cold and adrenaline were claiming most of her attention.

"On the count of three," Boris said. "One . . . two . . . *three!*" The flyer didn't budge.

"Just a moment," Melnori said. He crawled underneath it and fiddled with the controls, then took up his position again and said, "Try it now."

This time, the flyer tipped sideways. They grunted and shoved until it went over, the armored underside slapping down on the rocks with a loud clang.

The former passengers remained upside down where they had died. Melnori dragged them into the river and let the water carry the bodies away, then splashed the rocks until they were free of blood. The cold water didn't seem to affect him at all.

"What are you doing that for?" Boris asked him.

"If we remove the evidence, they may never know what happened here," Melnori said. "I would like Tien Camp to remain undiscovered."

When he was done, he climbed into the flyer and pulled up on a T-handle between the seats, and the vehicle floated into the air. "Yes," he said. "I think it's time we left for a while. Perhaps we could save some time if we met my resistance leader halfway." He looked over at Zofia again, that unreadable expression still on his face, and said, "I believe she will be more eager than ever to meet with you now."

Chapter 5

First Occupation

Haute left the cavern complex at first light, moving out with his old backpack over one shoulder and a Skaarj weapon and ammunition belt over the other. Ablee had walked with him as far as the cavern entrance, then wished him luck and turned back to start breakfast for the hundred and six residents of the caverns. The only person who knew exactly where he was heading was Ablee. He was also the only person who knew exactly why. Neither of them had ever said anything to anyone about the voice from the wreck in the cave. They had decided there was no point.

Besides, Haute almost didn't believe it had happened. Who else would?

Haute moved uphill from the cavern complex, passing with a wave the first guard, then moving silently onward. A number of hunting parties were already out in other valleys. And Haute also knew that Jeeie had four different groups fishing streams and lakes within a half day's hike of the cave. Feeding more than a hundred people two full meals a day required a constant supply of food. Luckily, the mountains had more than enough. And with Ablee's ability to stretch food, it was working.

But where would it all end?

How long could they keep going?

Was there a better way to fight the Skaarj?

Haute needed to know answers to those questions and others. And the voice from the crashed ship just might be able to help him. The voice had said it was built to guide the ship and those who asked. Well, Haute was going to ask for guidance. He figured it wouldn't hurt to try.

It took him most of the day to reach the rock on the side of the mountain where he and Ablee had split up those many months before. At one point along the trip he thought he had heard the faint sounds of a Skaarj transport, but that faded and was gone. Now, with three hours of daylight left, he was within a fairly short climb of the cave.

The sweat dripped off his forehead, and he stopped at the rock to fill his water bottle. As he was doing so, the voice in his head spoke for the first time in months.

You have questions?

"I do," Haute said out loud, moving back and sitting on the rock. "I will ask them when I arrive in the cave."

Space. Time. It has no distinction to me.

"Well, location means a great deal to me," Haute said. "I will ask my questions when I reach the cave."

The voice did not respond. Haute took that to mean understanding. The last thing he wanted was to be sitting on a rock in the middle of the forest for hours and hours while the voice took him on a tour of who knew where. He wanted to be inside, out of the sun and the wind, before that happened.

He finished drinking, then started the last, steep climb, above the tree line and up the ridge to the cave formed by the impact of an ancient spacecraft. A craft that now talked to him in what he called *the voice*.

Inside the mouth of the cave he dropped his pack and checked to see if anyone else had been there since his last visit. No one had. Not even an animal track.

He dropped down on a large rock, staring out over the slowly darkening sky. There were no clouds, and the sunset was painting only a faint pink in the upper levels. He retrieved his water bottle, took a long drink, then looked around.

"Voice, I need guidance."

His words echoed off the rock walls and died into the blackness at the back of the cave. Haute knew that down there, in that blackness, was the hulk of the old spaceship, smashed into a pile of useless junk. How the voice spoke from it, he had no idea.

I exist in all time, including the time you now reside.

"I wish I could say I understand," Haute said aloud, even though the voice came to him inside his head. "But I don't."

Understanding is not important. I only guide.

"Fine," Haute said. "I need guidance."

The rock walls and the sunset vanished.

He found himself sitting in the huge chair inside the crashed spaceship. Only this was during a period before the ship crashed. Or at least that's what he had understood the last time the voice had brought him here, because the ship seemed to be moving.

Around him the wonderful, triangle-shaped room was the same as on his first visit. Large consoles filled with lights and strange writing filled all three walls. On the two walls he faced in his oversized chair were pictures of stars streaming past. Or maybe those walls were windows, and those really were stars.

He couldn't tell. The only thing that was different was that there was no one in the other huge chair beside Haute this trip.

Haute took a deep breath of the stale, almost sour-tasting air, then asked his first question. "Would you guide me to where I will have the next major fights with the Skaarj?"

Instantly the room changed.

Vanished.

Haute stood on a hillside overlooking a castle. He didn't recognize which castle it was, so more than likely it was in the far south. It looked deserted. The entire scene seemed to be frozen in time, even though he could feel a slight breeze.

Around him the air was cooler, which meant more than likely that the time was in the fall. And it was just before sunrise, with the sky alight in bright pinks and purples.

He stood, letting the cool wind blow through his hair as he stared at the castle, hoping to recognize it.

Nothing happened.

No fight.

Simply nothing. Even though the wind was blowing, everything was just frozen in a moment just after sunrise.

Then the scene shifted again to another castle he didn't recognize. It was warmer, and the sunrise wasn't so brilliant this time. Again, no fighting.

Nothing.

Just another moment snapped out of time.

Then a third castle. The same thing. Three different

castles, all right before sunrise, a logical time to attack.

But when?

How soon?

Suddenly the scene switched a fourth time, and he was again hanging by thorn-covered vines from a round pole in the ground. Skaarj guards and Nali prisoners surrounded him, all watching.

The Skaarj seemed to be laughing. The Nali stood silently; many had their heads bowed in what felt like shame.

The pain in the vision instantly overwhelmed him, as he felt the flames lick up around his feet, burning his skin, seemingly from the inside out.

"I don't need this again," Haute said aloud, and instantly he was back sitting in the huge chair in the ship.

Even though he knew what he was having was a vision, he was breathing hard and sweating. The faint memory of the intense headache twisted at the back of his mind like a memory he desperately wanted to get rid of. And his feet actually felt raw where the flames had touched them.

He forced himself to take a deep breath and remember back to how he had asked the question. He had asked for the *location* of the fights. The voice had shown him locations, including his death scene again.

But what he really wanted to know was if the Skaarj were going to be defeated. "Would you show me my world, my people, two hundred years in the future?"

Instantly he was standing on a hillside, staring up at a beautiful floating city, with thin, delicate towers. Nothing in his wildest imagination could have brought forth such beauty. Flying ships moved between the city and the ground as easy as birds. There was no sign of the Skaarj at all.

Just Nali, living in a beautiful sky-city.

The immense relief overwhelmed him. He was going to die, of that he had no doubt. But they would defeat the Skaarj eventually.

He again found himself sitting inside the ship, staring out through the huge windows at the stars flashing past.

Your questions are imprecise.

Haute laughed out loud. "I know that. Should I have asked simply if the Nali will defeat the Skaarj?"

The answer to that question would be yes and no. Again imprecise.

"Yes and no?" Haute asked aloud, his joy at seeing a future clear of the Skaarj draining from him. "Can you guide me to the no you speak of?"

The scene shifted.

Now, Haute found himself standing on a barren hillside overlooking a tarydium mine. He could sense, without knowing how, that he was at a great distance in the future.

This scene was not frozen in a time. People moved. Airships flew overhead. Transports sped along smooth roads.

And the Skaarj were everywhere.

Next, he was inside a tarydium mine.

The Skaarj were using Nali and other strange-looking creatures for slaves in the mine. From what he could tell, the Skaarj had been there for a great number of years.

Haute, as if in a speeded-up vision, saw it all. The monsters had returned to his world, and this time they had won.

He wanted to shout no. That this wasn't the future for his people.

But he knew, deep down inside, that it was.

Yes and no.

Haute understood. The Skaarj had been defeated once. And had won once.

Yes and no.

The voice almost sounded insistent.

Haute found himself outside again, staring upward at the sky, at a streak of light that seemed to be falling. Another ship, crashing. He watched it smash into the ground, feeling the jarring of the earth for a distance around the site.

And then the events of the vision sped up, as if time were flowing like a raging river past his eyes.

It was a strange vision that he would always remember. A vision of a beautiful, crippled angel. And as the vision ended, Haute truly understood what the voice had meant by the answer to his original question.

Yes.

And no.

Chapter 6

Second Occupation

The Hhuman prisoners knew nothing. Karrikta decided that was the case when they failed to change their story even after he had eaten one of them alive, starting from the feet and working his way upward. They had screamed, they had regurgitated the contents of their stomachs, they had even attacked him with the waste sucker, but they had steadfastly clung to the story that they were nothing more than prisoners en route to a place called "Kira."

The one he was eating even tried to convince the others that they were *on* Kira. The prisoner was clearly delusional by then, but its adherence to the same story even under extreme stress was another argument for the truth of the tale.

Now, as he stood in his private office and allowed a delicate, furry Nelsian slave to lick off the remnants of his meal with its silky tongue, he tried to fit together the pieces of the puzzle. A Hhuman prison ship crashes—but right away he ran into questions. What was a prison ship doing so far away from Hhuman space? Karrikta had never even heard of a Hhuman before this. While it was entirely possible for a tarydium source as large as Na Pali to knock a passing ship out of hyperspace, that ship had to be headed past the planet in the first place, and Karrikta could see no reason why this one would come here if it was truly what its passengers said it was.

Also, the way they fought belied the Hhumans' claim just as badly. Prisoners wouldn't fight like that. Anyone who could kill as many battle-trained Skaarj warriors as they had would be running their home planet.

Unless the rest of their race was even tougher.

Impossible. A race that vicious would have taken over the galaxy by now.

The Nelsian finished with his chest and started licking his face, but its tickly tongue was too distracting. "Go away," he told it, and when it left his office he looked out the window while he thought. His office was only one floor below the command center; the sight of Rrajigar spread out below him always calmed his nerves. Clean streets full of slaves and overseers, all working hard at their little pieces of the bigger picture. The visual reminder of subjugation and order always helped him order his own mind.

Well, usually. While he looked at this city that had once belonged to the slaves, a crazy idea came to him: What if the violent members of Hhuman society were considered criminals? What if instead of running things, they were locked up and sent away? Weapons made great equalizers; it might be possible for non-violent people to capture violent ones if they worked together. Or maybe they could hire some of the criminals to catch the others. Either way, that might at least explain how a ship full of them could be so competent, while the species as a whole was not.

It was a difficult concept for him to grasp, but there were precedents. The Nali, right here on this planet, were so seldom violent that the few who were capable of it were shunned rather than revered. Except for one, of course, but that one was safely dead.

The Nali were proof that a society *could* function without aggression, just not very well.

But the Hhumans. . . . Either his prisoners were lying to him, which he could hardly believe, or they didn't know the whole story. Maybe their ship had come here for a reason that had nothing to do with them.

So someone else on board could blow up a tarydium mine?

The pieces didn't fit yet. Karrikta stood up and began to pace. He looked at the trophy heads on the wall, Nali and Kraal and Slith, and even a Skaarj he had defeated in a hand-to-hand duel, but they offered no insight. He walked up to the Skaarj—an old academy companion named Berggren—and pushed the button on the trophy plaque to play the vanquished warrior's last words.

"Beware of . . . pretense," the pain-wracked voice croaked out. "I nearly defeated you . . . with misdirection."

Karrikta had never been able to decide if that was honest advice or a last-minute practical joke. Knowing Berggren, it was probably both. It had worked, too. In the years since, Karrikta's fighting style had changed, slowing from the all-out berserk fashion he had used to defeat his academy mate to a more considered, methodical approach. All the same, he didn't see how the advice applied here, beyond the obvious wisdom of watching his back.

He moved to the Nali head, horribly scarred by the whip that now hung below it, but a timid knock at the door stayed his hand only inches from the replay button. He didn't need to push it, anyway; he knew the Nali's dying words by heart. "The avenging angel will bury you," it had said. He had always thought that an interesting threat, but it lacked the subtlety of Berggren's admonition. And it was equally useless here.

The knock came again. "What is it?" he growled. If someone was going to take the passive role even before they stated their business, they deserved an aggressive response.

An old Kraal, long past his usefulness as a warrior, opened the door and stuck his bumpy head around the jamb. "Excuse me for interrupting, sir, but we just intercepted another burst transmission from the Nali resistance. It came from the Sopiny station. We're still translating it, but it's clear that three more Hhumans have survived, and they have a Nali guide. The message seems to be making an arrangement with someone to meet with them at a coded location."

"Any idea where that location is?" Karrikta asked.

"The message just called it number twenty-three."

Karrikta's opinion of the resistance grew higher every time he encountered them. It had taken years before the Skaarj had detected a pattern in the static bursts that mysteriously reflected off the moons, and years longer to crack the encryption scheme just to find messages written in a dead language. They had put sensors on the moons and located the transmitters easily enough, and spies had watched their operators fish message bottles out of the river, but so far

Karrikta had left those ground stations unmolested, hoping to crack that last layer of encoding and begin tracking the resistance's movements. But now it looked like they were using code names within the coded language! Devious, devious.

But there was still useful information in the messages. Karrikta knew that the person who sent it was upstream from the transmitter, and that was all he really needed to know.

He still had security forces out looking for the Hhumans. "Tell the search parties to concentrate their forces on the Sopiny Canyon," he said.

"Yes, sir." The Kraal turned away to go back upstairs and relay his order, but in his haste to leave he bumped into another messenger—one of the Skaarj security team—and fell to the floor.

"Sorry, sir," he said, climbing slowly to his feet.

The Skaarj ignored him. "Commander," he said, "I just lost contact with two of our scouts in Sopiny Canyon. They were flying upriver and were moving in to investigate some activity on the bank when we lost their signal."

"Shot down?" Karrikta asked.

"No, sir. We're still receiving the transponder beacon. The flyer moved upstream a few paces shortly after the scouts stopped responding, stayed there for just a few minutes, then rose out of the canyon and headed south."

"Track it," Karrikta said, certain of whom it carried now. "You," he told the Kraal. "Move the searchers out of Sopiny and have everyone follow that flyer, but make sure they stay out of sight until I give the order to move in. With any luck, it'll lead us right to the head of the resistance."

The Kraal scurried away. Karrikta followed him

and the other Skaarj up the stairs a level into the command center, where he told a surveillance tech, "Get a visual on that flyer."

The tech said, "I'm trying, sir, but it's staying underneath the trees. I can show you where the transponder is coming from, but that's it."

"Do that."

The tech switched the view on his monitor from an electronic tracking grid to a visual image. Karrikta watched the treetops slide past on the screen. From overhead it was hard to tell how steep the terrain was, but it was certainly covered with vegetation. Occasionally, a glimpse of motion betrayed the presence of the flyer, but it was too small to make out any detail when that happened.

"Zoom in," Karrikta ordered.

The tech did so. Now the trees whipped past with dizzying speed, but the glimpses of the flyer offered tantalizing detail. He could make out three Hhumans and a Nali, all wedged into the space designed for two Skaarj. The Nali was driving.

Karrikta loved the heady rush of power he felt at times like this. He could destroy those four beings with a single command. A few words—his only cost would be a breath of air—and four lives would come to a fiery end.

The planet would be a safer place for the Skaarj if he gave that order, but therein lay the true thrill of command, for Karrikta knew that he *might* be able to make the planet even safer if he waited until they led him to more of their kind. They could easily betray the Nali resistance today, and maybe even provide some answers about these mysterious Hhumans. Yet it was a dangerous game. By killing them now he would sacrifice the possibility of greater gain, but by not killing them when he had the chance, he risked letting them escape to cause further trouble.

"Keep tracking them," he told the tech, then he turned away to arrange for a backup plan. That, too, was part of being a leader.

The weak link in the plan so far was the flyer itself. If the Hhumans abandoned it, Karrikta's security forces would lose their beacon. And the Hhumans *would* abandon it sooner or later; they couldn't very well fly into a resistance stronghold in a Skaarj flyer. So Karrikta had to figure out some way to track them after they went back to travel on foot.

"How many razorflies do we have in the area?" he asked. Imitation razorflies were a cheap, efficient way to camouflage a listening device. Real razorflies were so common, nobody paid any attention to one flying about.

Heads were raised up throughout the room. Another tech turned back to his monitor, tapped the controls until he found what he was looking for, and said, "Four, sir."

Karrikta waved his hands. "No, no, I don't mean just the immediate vicinity of the flyer," he said. "I mean in the area they're moving toward."

"Uhh, that's what I meant, sir."

Karrikta growled. "*Four* close-quarters surveillance drones in how much area?"

"There were more, sir, but they were all called in for the search near the Jenkraak mine."

"I see." Karrikta sighed. That had been his own order. Another of the little thrills of command: realizing in front of your subordinates that you'd made a mistake. "Well, send them back. Have them follow the flyer's path, and as soon as it stops moving, have them close in and follow the passengers."

"Yes, sir."

It would take time for them to catch up. A flyer—even one dodging tree trunks—was much faster than a razorfly.

What other mistakes had he made? This remote-control hunt irritated him. He itched to get out there in a flyer himself, or to simply track and kill his quarry on foot like a Skaarj warrior was meant to, but he had too much responsibility now to allow himself that pleasure. If something else happened while he was away, he had to be here to direct the response to it.

He remembered Berggren's advice. "Beware of pretense." Gladly, but who was pretending what here? That was always the question, wasn't it?

Chapter 7

First Occupation

Three short months after Haute had returned from his trip to the mountain, to talk to the voice, one vision came true.

He eased himself through the trees, careful to not make a sound, until he could see the castle Dnaltrop sitting tucked against the mountainside. The sun had not yet broken over the nearby peaks, and the ground was still wet with dew. The air had a chill to it that foretold of cold months ahead.

For a moment the image of the castle burned into Haute's mind as it overlaid with the image in his memory from the vision. Both were exact, right down to the feeling of abandonment coming from the castle.

Actually, Haute knew that feeling had real basis. All the captured inhabitants of Dnaltrop had been transported north, to work one of the mines there. Only six Skaarj stayed here to guard the castle and the mine. Mostly the mine. Since tarydium seemed to power the Skaarj transports, and the systems that kept the

Skaarj alive, they valued tarydium a great deal. Far, far more than the Nali had ever done. There were even rumors among the Nali that the Skaarj couldn't survive without tarydium in their suits. Haute wasn't so sure he believed that.

Haute gazed out at the castle and the open fields that framed it on three sides. Dnaltrop was the farthest castle to the south in the occupied Nali world. Haute and the other members of the Mountain Fighters council figured that it would be the best place to first attack the Skaarj and start driving them back north, toward their crashed ship. Haute had only told Ablee about the vision, but when he and Ablee had presented the idea to the rest around the late-night fire, they had all agreed it would be the best plan of attack.

Haute had not told Ablee about the vision of his own death. Or of the beautiful angel in the future. He figured there would be no point. At least at the moment.

Behind, and at Haute's left, eighteen armed Nali crouched in the trees and brush, waiting for his signal. He had wanted to be the one to give it, after he had seen the castle. He wanted to make sure it was the same as in his vision.

It was. The very same, right down to the grass growing up in the middle of what had once been a busy main road.

He turned to his brother, Bccui. "Go. And be careful."

Bccui nodded, the serious focus in his eyes never even allowing him to smile. He turned and motioned for five others to follow him. They all knew exactly where they were heading. They were going in a side door of the castle, one of the hidden entrances in this castle that was much like the hidden one Bccui and the rest of Haute's family had escaped from in another castle, far to the north.

Now, until Bccui got into position, they had to wait. Haute forced himself to take a deep breath and to check for the tenth time the charge of the rifle he carried. It was full, and so were the other ten in the belt over his shoulder.

He stretched his legs as best he could while crouched in the brush. His nerves were tight, as if every sense in his body was on high. Even the slightest twig snapping made his heart jump. To take his mind off the castle in front of him, he glanced around at the others.

Rentahs, the young fighter they had rescued from a Skaarj transport, was closest on his right. He had turned into one of their best fighters. And smartest. He looked as tense as Haute felt.

Targee crouched just beyond Rentahs, his gaze on the castle. Haute could never tell if he was nervous or not.

The few other fighters Haute could see looked nervous, but they were a good group, mostly level-headed and decent shots with Skaarj rifles. And most important, all hated the Skaarj and were willing to kill them.

Of the more than two hundred living in the cavern complex, there were fewer than thirty who knew, without a doubt, that they could fight. And another twenty who *weren't sure yet*.

Nali, as a people, were just not suited to fighting. It was something about his own people he had never realized. Of course, until the Skaarj came, the Nali had never been tested, or pushed in any fashion at all. In the last months since the Skaarj ship had crashed, that had changed a great deal for some. Haute didn't want to think about how it might be changing for those forced to work as slave labor in the mines.

A flash of a mirror near the castle wall told Haute that Bccui's team had found the entrance and were going inside. They would position themselves in hidden locations around the market area near the main boulevard, to get behind and cut down any Skaarj running from the mine toward the front of the castle.

Haute knew from Jeeie's scouts that one Skaarj guard was stationed near the front archway, just inside. The rest of the Skaarj spent their time near the back of the castle, where the entrance to the mine opened up off the main boulevard of the castle.

"Let's go," Haute said, just loud enough for those near to hear him. "Spread out and stay low."

Slowly, he moved more out into the open, staying on his hands and knees as he worked his way down the slight incline and then up toward the front archway of the castle.

Around him, the others spread out, two going very wide to the left, two wide to the right. Most of them moved through the brush and tall grass with the experience of mountain people, making almost no sound, and moving very few leaves.

Haute finally reached the edge of the main road leading from the castle. From this position forward, he would be completely in the open for the last fifty paces to the large archway.

He stopped and made himself really look at everything around him. Nothing unusual for the front of a castle. No traps that he could see. So far, the morning was calm and quiet. Not even a breath of wind.

His clothes were wet from the dew, and in the

nearby forest birds chirped. The sun had not yet cleared the tops of the trees, leaving the castle in shadow. Haute hoped that in a few minutes he would get the chance to see the sunrise.

In the back of his head, he could feel the slight headache starting to build from the tarydium sensitivity. He couldn't have a great deal of time inside the castle, that much was for sure. And neither could a number of the others with him. But fighters like Bccui and young Rentahs didn't have tarydium sensitivity problems. They would be able to stay for as long as it took to kill the Skaarj.

Haute raised up slightly and looked for his men. The two that had swung far to the right were now inching along the castle wall toward the gate. The two on the far left had just reached the castle wall, but were in close enough position to start. The others were in a fan formation around the archway, hiding in the tall weeds.

"Ready?" Haute asked the young Rentahs who crouched a few paces to his right.

Rentahs nodded, bringing his Skaarj rifle up into firing position and aiming it at the archway entrance.

Quickly, Haute slipped out of the ammunition belt and laid it in the grass, then put the Skaarj rifle on top of it, armed, charged, and ready to fire, just in case he needed to get back to it quickly.

He took a deep breath, then stood and walked five steps forward and slightly to the left, leaving the line of fire toward the main gate completely open for Rentahs. He stopped in the middle of the road, facing the castle.

They had decided that the best way to get the Skaarj guard out of the archway was to lure him out with a prisoner, who appeared to be coming in out of the mountains to give himself up. Then when the Skaarj had cleared the arch, Rentahs would kill him. And if Rentahs missed, Targee or one of the others would kill the guard, with luck, before the Skaarj shot Haute.

Ablee had complained bitterly about Haute using himself as bait. He had said that Haute was more valuable to the fighters alive than dead in the first major counterattack. Others had agreed with him, but Haute had waved off the objections by saying that there was no person who was too valuable to lose.

Actually, Haute had two reasons for being the target. One, he would never be able to live with himself if he ordered someone else to do it, and that person got killed. Second, if he was going to trust the visions and the voice in the cave, he knew where and how he was going to die. It wasn't by getting shot in front of an empty castle.

That, however, was if he trusted the visions.

He felt almost naked, standing there in the morning stillness outside the empty castle. The slowly growing headache warned him to turn and run. Get away.

Anywhere.

But he stayed solidly in the road and again forced himself to breathe. Then he shouted, "Anyone inside?"

His voice echoed through the gate and off the stone walls much louder than he had expected.

A moment later, a Skaarj guard eased around from behind the archway, his weapon pointed directly at Haute. The weapon looked far more natural in a Skaarj's hand than in a Nali's. Just a twitch of the finger and the Skaarj would cut Haute in half, spraying his blood back over the grass.

But Haute was gambling his life on the hope that

the guard was bored. And having a prisoner just might entertain for a few moments.

Haute raised his hands into the air, showing the guard that he had no weapon.

The guard hesitated a moment.

"Keep coming," Haute heard Rentahs in the grass behind him whisper at the guard. "Just a little farther out."

The Skaarj lowered his weapon slightly and stepped a little more into the open, just as Rentahs had asked for.

From Haute's right, a blue and green beam snapped out and caught the guard in the chest, smashing him into the air and backward. Before the guard even hit the ground, two more bursts of fire from two other locations behind Haute tore the guard completely apart, splaying the red Skaarj blood in all directions.

Haute felt frozen in relief as again time seemed to stand completely still.

Then he moved, ducking back into the grass and rolling to his weapon, all in seemingly slow motion.

The guard's body still flew through the air backward, slowly, seeming to take forever to land as Haute came up with the rifle in his hands, aiming at the front archway.

It had worked.

The Skaarj's body hit the stones, and suddenly time returned to normal for Haute.

The echo of the shots rang through the castle, and his relief instantly passed, replaced by a focus on the next stage of the castle attack.

They all waited.

Was there another guard near the front?

Haute had bet there wouldn't be. And the scouts had said there would be only one. But for the moment, everyone waited, unwilling to climb to his feet and head inside.

A long few seconds with nothing moving.

Finally, Haute stood again, weapon pointed at the front. "Take up positions inside!" he shouted, his voice echoing back off the forest.

Instantly, the others appeared from their hiding positions in the grass and ran for the archway, moving quickly to take up hiding positions in the main market area.

"Nice shot," Haute said, smiling at Rentahs as they ran behind the others.

"One down, five or six to go," Rentahs said as they passed under the castle archway and turned left, looking for any cover.

The market place had clearly been abandoned quickly. And some time ago. Weeds were growing up through the stones, and a layer of dust and dried mud coated everything that had been left in the open.

Rentahs ducked into the old guard booth while Haute found the remains of an old shop built against the outer stone wall. He ducked inside the open door into the black shadows, fighting to make his eyes adjust quickly.

The shop had been the work place of a tapestry maker. A number of bolts of cloth and boxes of thread littered the floor from a hasty search done months before. Haute made note to take as much from here as they could carry. It would come in handy for clothes and sleeping blankets in the caves.

Then he chastised himself for not thinking of bringing a support crew to haul salvageable items if they did take the castle. If this worked, and they decided to attack another castle, he would make sure to get the supplies from the castle next time.

He moved into the shadow near the door, where he could watch the main street and two of the side streets that flowed down into the main market area.

Suddenly, Rentahs appeared in the door and ducked inside. "I found this," he said, holding up a metal device the size of a rifle butt. "It's a Skaarj communication device."

A strange babble of speech and clicks came from the box in his hand. It was loud enough to echo through the entire market area.

Haute stared at it for a moment. The Skaarj near the mine were trying to contact the guard, more than likely to find out what the shots were about. When the guard didn't answer, they would come.

Haute also bet they were reporting to the main Skaarj forces to the north. Since the Skaarj had no air transport that Haute knew about, it would take them at least half a day by ground to reach this location from the nearest castle. There was time to win this fight and escape.

"Quickly," Haute said. "Throw it into the middle of the market area."

Rentahs instantly moved to the door and did as he was told. The metal box smashed on the stone surface and bounced a few times before coming to rest ten paces from the body of the Skaarj guard.

"You watch to the left," Haute said. "I'll watch the right. And don't fire until they've all entered the market area. We want Bccui's group to be behind them."

Rentahs nodded and crouched at the right of the door, watching down the streets on the left.

Haute stayed at the left of the door, guarding the right.

The next twenty seconds seem to stretch into hours, as again time changed.

Time, in Haute's visions in the mountain cave, cost him hours and hours of the real world, without seeming to take any time at all. Yet waiting like this for Skaarj to appear seemed to take hours and hours without really doing so.

Time was strange. Very strange.

"They're coming," Rentahs whispered, pulling his gun up to his shoulder and aiming it out the door to the left.

Haute saw nothing coming down the main boulevard, but one Skaarj was moving slowly from door to door down the right side street, sneaking up on the market area.

One on the left, one on the right. They were clearly moving as experienced fighters.

Haute's heart sank, and his stomach twisted into a tighter knot. He had hoped that the Skaarj would simply march down into the market to discover what the Skaarj guard had shot at. But clearly, that was not the case. The Nali Mountain Fighters had a real fight on their hands for the first time in the history of the Nali race.

Haute just hoped they were up to it.

"Wait until they're in the market," Haute whispered to Rentahs, then brought his own rifle up into position and tracked it on the slowly moving Skaarj on his side.

Then down the main boulevard, two more Skaarj moved, the forward one stopping and covering the other as he moved forward.

"Two on the main road," Haute whispered to Rentahs, who nodded back.

At almost the same time, all four Skaarj reached the market area. Two found positions near center booths while two others moved toward the body of the guard, more than likely to see what killed him.

"Take the one on the left," Haute whispered, pulling his rifle tight against his shoulder and letting out a long, slow breath. "I'll go for the right. On my mark."

Rentahs nodded.

"Now," Haute said, and pulled the trigger.

The pulse of the rifle kicked back in his hands as his shot hit the Skaarj directly in the chest, smashing him into the air and flipping him over backward.

Rentahs' shot did exactly the same to the other Skaarj.

Then, before the two remaining Skaarj could even turn to fire at Haute and Rentahs' position, a dozen other shots sliced the air of the market, smashing the two down from all directions.

So many energy beams hit the Skaarj that they both simply exploded, spraying blood and cloth and bones everywhere.

Then the shots cut off and the market was silent, the echoes of the killing fading off into the trees and nearby hills.

No one moved.

Haute didn't even lower his rifle.

After a few long seconds of deathly stillness, the Skaarj communication device broke the silence of the market area with the harsh sound of the Skaarj language. It seemed that either they still had a guard in front of the mine, or the Skaarj at another castle were trying to get in touch with this group. It really made no difference at the moment.

Haute lowered his rifle and stepped into the market.

The acid smell of blood and tarydium powder filled the air, seemingly swirled and twisted by the gentle wind.

Skaarj blood, not Nali blood. A very nice change.

As he moved from the dark of the old shop into the light of the market area, the sun colored the top spires of the castle with orange light, signaling a new day had begun.

A new day for the Nali, also. They had recaptured a castle. And even though they were going to leave it very shortly, the castle was theirs.

And so was the day.

Chapter 8

Second Occupation

Zofia clung to the seat and tried not to scream as tree trunks whipped past only inches from the side of the flyer. Twice, low-hanging branches had nearly clipped her in the head, but Melnori refused to take the flyer up above the treetops.

Wind whistled around the ragged edges of the canopy. It had shattered almost down to the dashboard when the flyer had landed upside down; what was left hardly protected the passengers from anything, even when they crouched low.

That was hard to do. The flyer had two wide seats designed for oversized Skaarj butts, but three people and a Nali was a tight fit. Especially since they had to give Melnori room to operate the controls. He wasn't all that good at it; it was clear that even though he understood the concept he hadn't had much practice.

"I really think we'd be better off it—look out!" A leaning tree loomed up in their path. Melnori yanked upward on the T-handle, tilting sideways at the same time, and the flyer lurched over the trunk, but that put them in the branches of another tree just beyond it. Leaves slapped at them, and the world became a blizzard of green, then they burst into clear air again, and Melnori brought them back down to skim along a few feet above the ground once more.

"Let me *drive*," Zofia demanded. She dug into the gap between her and Boris, drew her automag out of its holster, and held it to the Nali's skinny head.

"If you shoot me, we will be even more certain to crash," he pointed out, not slowing down a bit.

"Why is it so damned important that *you* drive?" she asked him.

"Because only I know where we are going."

"That doesn't make a damn bit of difference," she told him. "You can give directions, can't you?"

"Yes, but—" A wall of close-spaced tree trunks came at them. Melnori tilted the T-handle all the way to the right, and the air car tipped 90 degrees. The lower edge dug a deep furrow in the ground, throwing dirt up at them, then just as they passed between the trees, it slammed into a root and launched them into the air.

"Damn it, that's enough!" Zofia screamed as he brought them upright again.

"Shut up and let him drive," Gerick said. He was sitting between her and Melnori, and he seemed to be barely hanging on. In fact, the arm he had put around her shoulder bounced free with every dip and bump, and his hand kept creeping closer to her right breast.

She grabbed his fingers and wrenched them backward. "If you were interested in anything besides copping a feel, you'd—yeow!" One of the hollow geodesic bushes exploded around them.

"We're almost there," Melnori said. "Get ready to jump out. When you hit the ground, roll with the impact."

"You aren't going to stop?" Boris asked.

"No. The Skaarj are almost certainly tracking us. I am deliberately leaving a trail for them to follow, so it will tie up their resources looking for us. But if they see us stop, they'll know exactly where to search. So I'll drop you off in motion and continue until I can find a convincing place to wreck the flyer. Stay under cover nearby until I come back."

"You're crazy!" Zofia said. "We've left a path as clear as a highway; I'm not hanging out anywhere close to it. And if your precious leader is anywhere around here, you've put her in danger, too."

"She's not," said Melnori.

"Then why are we—"

Melnori slowed down. "Jump, *now!*"

The flyer was entering a grassy spot between trees, but nobody jumped. Melnori sighed and tilted the flyer sideways again, then rolled it completely over. Unlike the Skaarj soldiers, he was expecting the maneuver, and he reversed the thrust as it came around, holding them upside down a few feet above the grass.

It had been impossible to strap four people in. Only Melnori wore a harness; Zofia felt her grip on the seat loosen, and she barely had time to swing around and land butt-first, skidding to a stop on the soft grass.

Gerick rolled once, then flung his arms out and slapped the ground to stop himself.

Boris had been holding on to the unbuckled harness; he clung to it now, dangling beneath the flyer, his feet digging trenches in the ground while he struggled with Melnori for the controls. The flyer lurched upward, rotated to the left, then came down again just in time for Boris to fly backward into a bush. It yanked him free, then flung him back toward Zofia and Gerick. He landed running and managed to stay upright.

"'Shut up and let him drive,'" Zofia said, standing up and gathering her belongings, which were strewn all along the flyer's path. She looked upward and was pleased to see that the forest canopy completely covered the grassy meadow; at least they were safe from observation from above.

"He was good," Gerick said, dusting himself off. "If you hadn't been so panicked, you'd have seen that. I just didn't figure him for crazy."

"Yeah, well that shows what you know."

Boris came up and handed her pack to her. "You all right?" he asked.

"Yes. You?"

"Yeah."

She laughed. "You looked like Tarzan or something, hanging onto that strap. What were you thinking? Avenging angel?"

He blushed. "I thought maybe I could hold on. I didn't really have time to think it over beyond that."

"Sure."

"I'm fine, too," Gerick said in the tone of someone who hasn't been asked.

"Leg okay?" Zofia asked belatedly.

He stood up and tested it. "Still weak, but I didn't break it again."

"Good."

He pointed at Zofia's pants. "You've got grass stains on your ass."

She brushed off what she could. "So what now?" she asked. "Do we wait for the bastard or not?"

"I say, screw him," said Boris. "I didn't trust him much before this, and now—"

"Do you want off this damned planet?" Gerick asked. "Like it or not, he's the only ticket we've got at this point. So unless you've got a better plan, I'd suggest gathering up our stuff and finding a good shade tree to hang out under until he gets back."

Zofia didn't even try to hide her surprise. This was Gerick talking? Then she remembered Melnori's promise to heal his ankle. If she were stranded on an alien planet with a broken leg, maybe she would accept whatever help was offered, too.

So they carried their belongings a few dozen yards away and hid behind some bushes until they heard him walking back toward them.

"Over here," Zofia called out when she was sure it was Melnori.

He sauntered over, one pair of hands in his pockets and the other pair crossed over his chest. "Sorry about the sudden roll," he said, "but that was the only soft landing site I knew of, and I couldn't really turn back for a second pass."

Zofia didn't trust herself to say anything civil. Apparently, neither did Boris.

Gerick broke the silence. "So, take us to your leader," he said.

Melnori nodded. "Very well, follow me."

He led the way westward, deeper into the mountains. Gerick was still hobbling on his crutch so they moved slowly, but they had gone a mile or so when Melnori held up his hand and said, "I believe we are on the path she must travel to reach Tien Camp."

Zofia looked around. She could see no sign of a path, only more of the same dense forest in every direction.

"Are you sure?" she asked.

Melnori looked at her and shrugged his multi-shouldered shrug. "It would probably not be wise for alien beings to surprise her. Why don't you three wait under that tree over there—" he pointed to a shady spot beneath a huge, old gnarled tree with wide-spreading limbs "—and I'll wait here until she comes by."

"How do you know she hasn't already done that?" Boris asked.

Melnori reached out between two trees and plucked at a spider web. "No one has traveled here today."

"What about twenty feet over? What makes you so sure she would come right through here?"

Melnori pointed off to the south. "What do you see?" he asked.

"Trees," Boris said. Zofia stepped up beside them and looked in the same direction. Sure enough, there were big-trunked trees as far as she could see, which was pretty far when she came to think about it. There seemed to be a tunnel of overarching branches leading off into the distance from right where she stood. She turned around and looked to the north, and sure enough, it extended that way, too, up and over a little rise in the ground.

"You've cleared out a covered highway?" she asked.

"We grew it, actually," Melnori said. "This forest wasn't that densely overgrown until we planted it about eighty years ago. We wanted to make it harder for the Skaarj to move through, just in case we needed to hide. But we left corridors where we could move quickly ourselves when we needed to. This one leads almost directly to Tien Camp; I'm nearly certain Ranel will use it today."

"And if she doesn't?"

"Then we have a long walk ahead of us. But don't worry; I know Ranel. She will be coming through here in a flyer as soon as she gets my message."

Zofia wished she shared his conviction, but she had to admit that this was one of the more pleasant places she'd ever waited for a ride. She and Boris and Gerick settled in for lunch under the big tree that Melnori had pointed out, while he sat down cross-legged in the middle of the "road." Zofia hoped the Fearless Leader drove more carefully than he did, or he could wind up smeared across the front of her flyer.

A full stomach and the warm afternoon air made Zofia's eyes grow heavy. She knew she was dreaming when she found herself back in Inuit Corporation's starship design lab, downloading the plans for their hot new battleship. She didn't know whom she was working for, and she didn't really care; the up-front money alone had been worth the price of the job, and there was that much more waiting when she delivered the goods to her contact.

It seemed like a lifetime ago. Now, she was in a place where money didn't matter at all, and starships rained down out of the sky like hailstones.

"She's here," Melnori said.

Zofia opened her eyes and saw him standing over her. Beside him stood another Nali, not appreciably different from him in appearance. The resistance leader had the same tall, willowy appearance, the same double arms, the same flat chest. Melnori had called her "she," but if there were secondary sex characteristics among their race, they weren't obvious. An old, battered flyer bobbed lightly in the air a few yards behind her, still powered up for a fast getaway.

"Hi," Zofia said, standing up. "I'm Zofia." She held

71

out her hand, but the Nali either didn't know about shaking or didn't trust her yet.

Gerick and Boris stood up, too, and offered their names but not their hands.

"Ranel," said the leader. "Melnori tells me you want off Na Pali."

"Doesn't everyone?" Zofia asked.

"Some of us just want the Skaarj off Na Pali. Melnori says you've agreed to help us do that."

Zofia shrugged. "Maybe. It's not really our fight. Besides, I don't know how much use three more people will be."

"One person would be enough, if it were the right person," said Ranel.

"Yeah, right. Melnori gave us the history lesson."

Gerick spoke up. "He also says he can heal my busted leg. Let's see you deliver on that before we join any crusades."

Ranel looked at the three humans. She walked over to her flyer and took a boxy gadget out of it, then came back and waved it around at them and at their backpacks. Multicolored lights blinked on the display.

"What are you doing?" Zofia asked her.

"Checking you for homing devices."

"Find any?"

She frowned, looked up into the tree, then back at her detector. She waved it around again, then said, "No, I guess not." She looked at Melnori and said, "You're sure this is worth the risk?"

"I've seen them fight," he said. "They're ruthless."

"I hope you're right. We're going to have to strike soon, before the Skaarj take vengeance for the ones these three killed." She gestured toward the flyer and said to Zofia, "You've forced our hand. You might as well come see what you've pushed us into. Once you learn what we have planned, you can decide whether or not to join us."

This flyer at least had a cargo space behind the seats, but its bubble top was still intact, so Boris and Zofia had to crouch down over the backpacks while Gerick got in front with Melnori and Ranel. Zofia looked back into the clearing as Ranel drove away, making sure she hadn't left anything behind, but the grass under the tree was clean.

She spotted one of those nasty four-winged bug-birds on a branch right over where she had been napping. The hair on the back of her neck raised up when she saw it. She hated stinging insects; the thought that she had slept right beneath one the size of her hand made her skin crawl.

It seemed to sense her discomfort, and like the perverse creature it was, it dropped off its branch and swept toward the flyer. It came right up to the bubble and landed on it. Zofia reached over to close the tilt-out window, but it merely excreted on the glass and flew away. A moment later Ranel shoved the flyer's T-handle forward, and they swept away down the long tunnel of trees.

Chapter 9

First Occupation

Haute and young Rentahs worked their way slowly toward the tarydium mine entrance at the back of the castle, using each door, each building edge, as cover as they advanced up the castle's main boulevard, leap-frogging one ahead of the other as they had seen the Skaarj do. Around them, the early morning sun was cutting the chill in the air, lighting the tops of the castle towers with bright light.

Two other Mountain Figher teams, one led by Haute's brother, Bccui, the other by Targee, were working their way toward the mine, down the two side streets that ran parallel to the main boulevard.

The rest of the attack team was busy scrambling through the market stores to find and salvage anything any of them thought would be useful to the cavern community, and that they could carry on the day-and-a-half hike back. They were moving the goods to a secure location in the trees, just to get them out of the castle in case Skaarj arrived sooner than expected.

Haute's headache was now growing quickly. Without all the people using tarydium in the castle, he was lasting longer than he had in his own home castle. But from the way the headache was starting to slowly pound in the back of his head, he knew he didn't have much more than fifteen minutes, especially close to the mine.

Haute watched as Rentahs ran toward an open door, out in the open for a short distance. Suddenly, a pulsing explosion of Skaarj weapon fire cut through the air, smashing the building right above Rentah's head. Dust and rock splinters flew everywhere.

Haute ducked, shielding his eyes with two hands.

Rentahs managed to dive and roll into a doorway, out of the line of the Skaarj's fire.

Haute hadn't managed to get an exact spot on the Skaarj's location, since it was just around a slight corner. He was going to have to move forward, try for the alcove of the next door twenty paces ahead. Maybe from there he could get a shot off.

But just before he was about to run, Rentahs shouted, "Stay there! I can get an open shot."

Rentahs stood in the open doorway and pressed his back against the wall, taking deep breaths.

"You all right?" Haute shouted across the wide street.

"Fine," Rentahs said. "And I've got a clear shot if someone can distract him."

Before Haute even had time to think about a distraction, two shots echoed through the castle buildings. The blasts hit rock, exploding near the mine entrance, just out of Haute's sight. Bccui and his partner must have fired on the Skaarj guard.

Perfect distraction, and Rentahs knew it.

The young fighter didn't even hesitate. He swung

out onto the sidewalk, completely exposed to the Skaarj, raised his rifle and then fired.

To Haute, it seemed as if the kid was moving faster than the eye could follow, as if he'd practiced the move over and over.

Rentahs held his position for a long moment after firing, then lowered his rifle and took a long, deep breath, letting it out in a clear sigh.

Haute moved out into the street, rifle up in firing position, staring toward the front of the mine. A Skaarj lay dead near the mine entrance.

Nothing else moved.

"Nice shot, again," Haute said, moving over and patting the young fighter on the back. "You hurt?"

Rentahs shook his head no. "Just shaken is all."

"Well, take your time," Haute said, "and relax a minute. My guess is we've got at least two hours before any Skaarj can arrive. More than likely, we have far more time than that."

"I'll be fine," Rentahs said. "Thanks."

Haute watched as the kid took another long breath and let it out. He was already a great fighter. Maybe the best they had. Today alone, he had killed three of the few hundred Skaarj on the planet.

Up the street, Bccui and two of the other Mountain Fighters were stripping the weapon and ammunition belt from the dead Skaarj while Targee stood guard.

"Come on," Haute said to Rentahs. "We need to search for weapons and supplies."

"And close the mine," Rentahs said as they walked toward the entrance in the side of the mountain.

"What?" Haute said, not really understanding what Rentahs had said through his pounding headache.

"The Skaarj are guarding the mine," Rentahs said,

pointing ahead at the rock entrance. "And having our people work the mines for them as slaves. We close the mine and they lose whatever value they see in holding it."

Haute could see the young fighter's point, but the method of closing a mine carved out of solid rock was beyond him. Especially with the headache starting to cloud his thinking.

"Suggestions on how we might accomplish that task?" Haute said.

Rentahs shrugged. "I have a couple, but none that I'm sure will work." Then Rentahs smiled, one of the very few times Haute had seen him do so.

"We might," Rentahs said slowly, "if we're lucky, and do it just right, kill a few Skaarj when we close it."

"I like the sound of that," Haute said.

As they reached the body of the Skaarj, Haute glanced down at the monster, the red blood flowing into a pool on the rock, his huge claws lying useless against the stone. Rentahs' shot had caught the monster in the very center of the chest, right below the neck. Perfect. The kid clearly knew what he was doing.

Bccui, Targee, and the other fighters had gathered around the body. One had the Skaarj's weapon over his shoulder while another had the ammunition belt.

"Sensitivity getting bad, huh?" Bccui asked, putting his hand on Haute's shoulder.

Haute nodded and glanced at the mine. "Just too close, I guess. But I can last a few more minutes."

Bccui nodded, but didn't move his hand from Haute's shoulder, giving him both physical and mental support.

Haute glanced around the Skaarj guard's post.

"Search the area around this point and every room near here. Find where they were living. And if they've stored any extra weapons."

Without questions, Targee and two fighters turned and spread out, leaving Rentahs and Bccui with him.

Haute then turned to face the young fighter, pushing the headache back for a minute longer. "I'm willing to listen to some ideas."

Rentahs glanced at the rock opening into the mine and nodded. Then, as if target practicing, he raised his rifle, picked a spot on the rock wall just above the mine entrance, and fired.

The rock shattered as Rentahs held down the rifle's trigger, pouring the energy beam from the Skaarj's weapon toward one point. Suddenly a large explosion shattered the area, causing all three of them to duck.

A moment later a large chunk of rock smashed downward, sending clouds of choking dust in all directions.

Bccui helped Haute move back out of the cloud and a short distance away from the front of the mine. By doing that, it was as if a slight bit of the pressure in his head was released.

The three of them stood in the boulevard for a few seconds to let the wind sweep the rock powder and dust away. As the air cleared, it became obvious to Haute, staring at the pile of rubble, that Rentahs' method just might be able to close the mine.

His method and a little added explosive, placed in just the right place.

Haute turned to Bccui. "I'm going out to the hill. You two help with the search for weapons and then join me."

Bccui nodded.

"And when you search," Haute said, glancing up at

the rock above the mine entrance. "Also search deep in the mine. See if you can find some of the explosives used by our people to expand the mine before the occupation."

"You think there might still be some in there?" Bccui asked, surprised at the thought.

"The Skaarj just may have underestimated us," Haute said. "Why would they move it?"

Rentahs smiled at Haute. "I will search for it."

"No more than an hour," Haute said, fighting with the last of his will to keep the intense pain back. "On the hill outside."

Without waiting for a response, he turned and did his best to walk normally down the middle of the main street of a castle he had just captured.

The time on the hill, at a distance from the captured castle, cleared almost all of Haute's headache. In the hour since they had killed the last Skaarj, his men had managed to find a large number of supplies that were needed back at the caverns. It was going to be a job carrying them, especially since they had to make sure that no Skaarj could track them to the caverns. There was no doubt the next two days were going to be long. But returning successful from a mission was going to make it worthwhile.

"Look what we found," Bccui said, smiling as he came through the trees to find Haute. In his hands was a very heavy-looking wooden box. Inside were long sticks of explosives used in the mining of tarydium. Rentahs also had a box and a roll of fuses slung over his shoulder.

"Great," Haute said, inspecting the contents of both boxes. This find was going to cause the Skaarj more grief than they could ever imagine.

"Come with me." He took one stick and headed back through the trees toward the open area in front of the castle.

He told Bccui and Rentahs to wait at the edge of the forest while he moved out fifty paces to a mound in the open. There he stuck the explosive stick in the ground, top up, and quickly returned to his companions' side.

"Rentahs," Haute said, "can you hit that stick with a short blast?"

"Easily," Rentahs said, swinging his rifle into firing position.

The next moment, he fired, the pulse of the energy beam echoing over the open space. The beam caught the explosive stick, and suddenly everything seemed to explode around them.

Haute was knocked backward onto his butt, and an instant later dirt and small rocks rained down on him, as if the heavens and earth had been turned upside down.

His ears were ringing and his headache was back, not so much from his sensitivity, but from the huge explosion.

"Amazing," Bccui said, standing and coughing as he brushed himself off.

"Everyone all right?" Haute asked, as the rest of his men came running from the area of the supplies, weapons drawn, to find out what had just exploded.

"Fine," Rentahs said, climbing to his feet and brushing off his arms before blowing the dust and dirt off his rifle.

"Guess we need to be a little farther away next time, huh?" Haute said, shoving himself to his feet. "That stuff is even more powerful than I had heard."

A huge cloud of dust drifted away from them on the

wind, exposing a large hole in the ground where the mound had been a few moments before.

"I'd say we have just found ourselves a new weapon," Haute said.

"No argument from me," Bccui said. "How about seeing if anyone with us has had experience with this stuff? Before we kill ourselves instead of the Skaarj."

"Good idea," Haute said, laughing. "Real good idea."

Chapter 10

Second Occupation

Melnori loved the sight of the forest sweeping past. For the moment, at least, he could pretend they were simply rushing deeper into the mountains rather than rushing headlong into battle with the Skaarj.

He hadn't been back to the stronghold for months. It was too risky for an advance scout to make regular trips. No matter how many precautions you took, you never knew when you were being followed, and you never knew what sort of welcome awaited you. Strongholds had been raided before, then left as traps for returning scouts.

The Dewei Refuge, however, had survived for centuries. It had been the headquarters for the old resistance when the Skaarj had first invaded, and it had never fallen into enemy hands in all the years since. Its location was part of the reason—the south end of the Begorn Mountains held no tarydium reserves, so there was nothing there of interest to the Skaarj—but vigilance had played just as big a part.

Information came in by coded radio burst, information went out through an underground river, and people came and went from different locations every time.

Ranel drove them to Roveld Lake, a long, deep lake surrounded by high mountains on all sides. "Make sure your windows are sealed," she warned, and when Melnori checked and assured her that they were, she plunged the flyer straight into the lake. The humans gasped, and even Melnori felt himself stiffen as icy blue water splashed up over the windshield. Bubbles made vision impossible for a moment, then they cleared away to reveal shafts of sunlight illuminating a lake bottom littered with boulders and waterlogged trees.

Then a dark shape loomed out of the distance. Ranel steered around it, and as it swept past on the left, they could see that it was a decayed spaceship. By the looks of it, it had been there for millennia. It was just a skeleton now, with bright yellow fish swimming in and out through the ribs. A six-tentacled squid had taken up residence in an engine nozzle. It reached out toward them, but retreated when Ranel flashed the headlights at it.

Melnori had seen this ship from above once, looking down into the lake from a ridgetop, but this was a new vantage.

Ranel paid it no attention. She steered for the deepest part of the lake, the canopy creaking under the pressure, then she aimed the flyer at a dark section of underwater cliff.

"Uh, Ranel?" Melnori asked as the moss-covered rock loomed closer.

"What?"

"Ranel, the cliff. The cliff!"

Just then she flipped on the lights, and the flyer slid smoothly into a round cave. Smooth rock walls slid past only a few feet on either side of the flyer.

"There're caves all through these mountains," she said. "You know that."

Melnori took a deep breath. "Yes, but I didn't expect one in the middle of an underwater cliff."

"There wasn't always a lake here, you know. Just a stream in the bottom of a canyon. Then the ship landed, and apparently its repulsors caused a big slide that buried half the ship and damned the river. Part of the cave flooded, so we widened a couple of passages for hidden entrances."

She flew them slowly along, nudging fish out of the way until the tunnel angled upward, bringing them out into air. The tunnel spiraled around, always rising, until they broke out into a huge underground chamber filled with other flyers, wheeled ground vehicles, trailer-mounted force cannon, and other instruments of war. It was lit by two bright sunglobes suspended from stalactites, and it went on and on. Melnori started to count the vehicles but lost track somewhere after fifty, and that was only a fraction of the equipment in the cavern.

"Where did all this come from?" he asked. He didn't ask why he hadn't been told about it before now; the less he knew about the resistance, the less he could betray if he were ever caught.

Ranel laughed. "Where *didn't* it come from? The resistance has been collecting this stuff since before either of us was born. It looks impressive until you realize this is nearly half of all our military capability. When we go up against the Skaarj, we'll need every bit of it and more." She looked back to Zofia and Boris. "The 'more' bit is where you come in."

"How so?" Zofia asked.

"We're going to attack Rrajigar. That's one of the Skaarj's major fortresses. If we can take that, we'll gain access to enough new weaponry to take another fortress, and so on all the way around the planet."

"But—but—" Melnori stuttered, "but I didn't get the city plan for you."

"One of the other scouts did. We've got all the information we need to attack. Come with me; I'll show you the rest of our preparations." To Gerick, she said, "And we will fulfill our promise to you."

If the humans were as astonished as Melnori at the arsenal the resistance had collected, they didn't betray it. Perhaps they didn't realize just how un-Nali-like it was to gather so many destructive weapons, or how many people had undoubtedly died to procure them. As Ranel led the way through them to a door on the far side of the cavern, Melnori realized that everything was of different design, probably scavenged from starships decades, even centuries, old. Each weapon would have different capabilities and limitations—it would be a nightmare to coordinate a battle with them all.

But it would be a nightmare to defend against them, as well. Every time the Skaarj thought they had figured out what was hitting them, something new would come along.

Dewei Refuge was mostly natural cavern, with tunnels bored between chambers and floors leveled to make footing more convenient. Stalactites still hung from the curved walls and ceiling, and sound echoed down the corridors from long distances away. Ranel led the way from the arsenal into another, circular tunnel, which in turn led to sections of the stronghold that Melnori was more familiar with from earlier visits. He knew when they passed the cafeteria just by the aroma; that meant the hospital would be just down the way.

That was where Ranel was taking them. Gerick limped along with them, his crutch clunking solidly on the rock floor with every other step, until they crossed through an arched doorway into the examination room. "Holy shit," he whispered when he saw the extent of it. It wasn't as big as the arsenal, but it was big enough, and it was filled with monitoring equipment, diagnostic tools, and treatment devices of every description, plus dozens of technicians tending them.

"We don't just collect weapons," Melnori said proudly.

One of the technicians came up to the group. His green tunic bristled with portable sensors that would have told him everything he wanted to know, but he assessed the situation without their help. Noting the crutch, he asked Gerick, "Broken internal skeletal support?"

"My leg, yes," he replied.

The tech crooked a finger. "Come with me."

Melnori said, "His friends would like to see the process."

"Certainly. All of you are welcome."

The tech led the way through the exam room into one of the major-wound treatment rooms, pausing just long enough at one of the diagnostic stations to check Gerick's tissue type with a protoplasmeter before proceeding.

The gentle patter of splashing water met them at the door to the treatment room. Inside was a wide pool with a jet of water spraying upward from one side and arching over to break into droplets that rained back down onto the surface.

"Please take off your garments and step into the pool," said the tech.

Gerick laughed. "I know I need a shower, but how's this going to help my leg?"

"The fountain has healing properties," the tech said.

Gerick looked over at Zofia and Boris and rolled his eyes. Zofia shrugged her shoulders, and Boris showed his teeth in the grin that Melnori had learned meant, "The joke's on you." Clearly, they had expected something a bit more technological.

"Our people are not backward," he told them. "We simply do not manufacture weapons. We have made considerable progress in other areas, most notably medicine. The fountain is more powerful than it looks."

Gerick said, "Whatever you say," and began pulling off his clothing. He tossed his shirt to Zofia, who caught it and set it down on the bench beside her, a look of distaste on her face. He kept handing her his shoes and socks and pants and undershorts until he was naked, even though it was clear she didn't want to touch them. Melnori didn't understand her reluctance—her clothing was just as soiled as Gerick's—but there was clearly more going on between them than a simple receiving of garments.

Gerick's smooth brown skin was covered with colorful designs. Melnori had seen the edges of them before, but most of the designs had been under his clothing until now. Must be a remnant of an ancestral color scheme for attracting mates, he supposed. Or perhaps protective markings; one of the designs on his back looked like a fierce snake, and one on his arm looked like a skull. Melnori had seen similar patterns on wild animals.

The technician steadied Gerick while he stepped over the fountain's low rim.

"Yow, it's cold!" Gerick shouted, his voice echoing in the tiled room.

"Oh, I'm sorry," the tech said. "Your body temperature is higher than ours. I will adjust it." He tapped a panel on the wall, and it lit up; then he slid his finger up a yellow scale. "How is that?"

"Better."

Melnori could feel the heat emanating from the fountain. Too hot for him, but apparently humans liked it that way.

Gerick stepped in with both feet and shuffled carefully over until he stood beneath the falling water.

"So how exactly is this supposed to heal my leg?" he asked.

"How much molecular biology do you understand?" the tech replied.

"Not enough to be dangerous. Forget it. At least I can get clean." Gerick held his face up to the spray and rubbed his hands over it, then proceeded to bathe himself. When he reached his crotch he wiggled the fleshy parts there at Zofia, but she turned red and looked away. Melnori was about to ask what was the matter when Gerick suddenly stopped and said, "Hey, it's eating my tattoos!"

Melnori didn't know what he meant at first, but when he realized that Gerick was looking at his arms and stomach, he saw that the designs there were fading. So were the ones on his back.

"You sons of bitches!" Gerick shouted, thrashing his way out of the pool. He stomped out onto the dry tile and shook off what water he could, but it was too late. His skin was the same smooth brown everywhere now.

"You had no right to—" he shouted, but then he stopped in mid-rant and looked down at his leg. He took a careful step, then put his entire weight on it. "Son of a bitch," he said in an entirely different tone of voice than he had used a moment ago.

"It's healed?" asked Zofia.

"Feels like it."

"You should spend at least twice as much time under the fountain as you have," said the technician, "but I'm sure you are substantially stronger now than you were."

"After one *minute?*" asked Boris.

Gerick looked at his arms, then bent his head around to look at his shoulders and back.

"They're all gone," said Zofia.

"Shit." He looked at the technician. "You have any idea how much trouble those were to have done? And how expensive?"

"I'm sorry," the tech said. "I didn't realize the designs were artificial. If I had known, I could have programmed the fountain to ignore your skin." He peered at the control panel, then added, "But you may be interested to know that the fountain healed two precancerous melanomas in your left forearm. One of them would have become malignant in less than a year. Perhaps that will make you less angry?"

Gerick looked at him with narrowed eyes. "You're shittin' me."

"Whatever that means, I suspect the answer is no, I am not."

Zofia laughed. "I'd call it a fair trade," she said. "Besides, that was the ugliest snake I'd ever seen."

"It was a wolf eel," Gerick snapped. He stared at her for a moment, then turned around and stepped back into the pool.

When the technician told him he could come out again, he looked like a completely different being. He stood straighter, he seemed more alert—everything about him looked refreshed and rejuvenated. Melnori knew that feeling; he took a healing shower every couple of years whether he needed it or not just to feel the rush.

As Gerick toweled himself off, he said, "That was better than drugs."

"Much faster, at least," Melnori told him.

"No, I meant . . . aw, forget it."

Zofia looked at him, then at the fountain. The tech caught her obvious interest and said, "If you have injuries as well, you are welcome to use it."

She blushed. Melnori didn't understand why, but she leaned close to the technician and whispered into his ear.

"Ah, yes," he said. "I see. No, that shouldn't be a problem. I can program it to leave those sites unaffected."

Boris and Gerick both looked at her, then Gerick suddenly burst out laughing. "Boobs! You're afraid you'll lose your boob job!"

"Shut up," she told him. Then she turned to the tech again and said, "Something's wrong. It didn't fix his brain; he's still a jerk."

Chapter 11

First Occupation

Haute picked Rentahs and Bccui to stay behind with him, then sent Targee with the rest of the men on their way home. Targee would make sure, in numbers of ways, that they were not followed to the caverns, even though they were all loaded down with supplies. Haute trusted them to get the supplies, including almost two boxes of the explosive sticks, back to the caverns.

He also trusted his brother, Bccui, and Rentahs to be the best at the plan they had come up with. They were going to attack, and with luck, wipe out the Skaarj that would be arriving shortly. From the scouting reports Haute had received, the Skaarj would send at least five from the two closest castles, moving in from other castles replacements for the ones that had left.

Of course, all that might change after today. But Haute doubted it would change much. There just weren't enough Skaarj on the planet to control everything with great numbers. That was their one large weakness. Their low numbers, and the fact that they *wanted* to control everything.

"You sure you're up to going back near the castle?" Bccui asked.

"No problem," Haute said. "As long as I don't go near the mine." And he was telling his brother the truth. The headache was now only a faint ache in his neck.

"Ready?" Bccui asked the young Rentahs.

"As ever." Rentahs held up five of the explosive sticks and patted his rifle.

"Okay," Haute said. "We're going to have to do this fast. It has been an hour and a half since we attacked. Replacements might arrive within the next thirty minutes."

Both Bccui and Rentahs nodded.

"We'll meet back here as quickly as we can," Haute said. "After it's over. Good luck."

Without another word, they both turned and headed at a quick run out of the trees and toward the left side of the castle. There was a trail there that led up into the rocks on the hillside above the mine. They were going to plant ten of the explosive sticks on that hillside, in places that they could see, and hit with a shot, from a distance. With luck, it would bring down enough of the hillside to block the mine, and maybe kill some Skaarj under the rock slide.

If they were lucky.

Haute's job was different. He turned and at a run headed for the front archway of the castle, also with ten explosive sticks in his hands. He was going to plant them around the entrance where he or Rentahs could hit them with a shot from the hillside. The

Skaarj that weren't under the rocks near the mine might head out of the castle and get caught in blasts at the front gate.

Or at least, that was also the plan.

Haute had no idea how it would really work. And he could just hear Ablee's voice in his head, yelling at him for risking his own life on complete foolishness. But Haute didn't feel that his life was so special. And again, he trusted the visions he had seen. He wasn't going to be lucky enough to die here today.

As he had done at his own castle as a kid, he climbed up the rocks of the main arch to plant three of the sticks in cracks in the rocks on both sides. He managed to do it, but only after breaking out into a complete sweat.

He finished and stepped back, making careful note of where each stick was. When hit with a shot from a Skaarj rifle, the resulting explosion would, without doubt, destroy the beautiful front of the castle. But it could be rebuilt, if and when the Skaarj had been defeated.

He then planted one explosive stick just above head height, fifteen paces to the right of the archway. And another in the same position on the left. His last two sticks he hid in distinctive-looking bushes about fifty paces from the front of the castle, one on each side of the road.

Then he retreated back to the hillside, and he checked his rifle to make sure it had a full charge and hadn't gotten jammed with dirt. It hadn't.

He was ready.

He had no idea if Bccui and Rentahs were also in position. He wouldn't know until he heard the sound of their gunfire and the resulting explosions. They had, with luck, both found good hiding places up on the hillside, where they could see the castle below, and the tops of the explosive sticks they had planted.

He settled down in the shade of a pine tree to wait.

Almost as if in his imagination, a faint rumble echoed over the warm morning. Slowly, the rumble got louder and louder. A Skaarj transport in the distance. They were on the way, right on time.

He again checked his weapon, then moved around behind the tree and down in a dark shadow, protected on three sides by rocks and a tree stump.

The rumble of the Skaarj transport now seemed to fill the entire area. Then, before it appeared, it seemed to grow softer. There was no dip in the road there. No more trees than normal to shelter and change the sound.

Then, just as quickly as the sound had died down, it increased again, louder than before. A moment later the transport appeared in the open area, a cloud of dust behind it. There was one driver and five others in the back. A total of six in the vehicle.

The change in sound meant the transport had stopped, just before reaching the open area around the castle. Stopped, no doubt, to let off troops. If the number of Skaarj were consistent with the scouting reports he had gotten from Jeeie, there were now at least four more on foot.

The transport moved down to a flat area in front of the castle and stopped, shutting down just short of where Haute had planted the two explosive sticks in the brush. The sudden quiet echoed through the trees, seeming to flood back into the space the noisy Skaarj vehicle had pushed it out of.

The Skaarj on board climbed out, weapons at the

ready. They quickly moved into positions on either side of the transport, using it as shelter.

Behind him, Haute heard brush cracking.

Skaarj were coming in through the trees toward the castle. And from what he could tell, one was twenty paces to his left.

More brush cracking came from his right. Another Skaarj was about fifty paces in that direction.

He was completely surrounded.

He forced himself to breathe very slowly as he crouched as low as he could and stayed completely still. He had discovered many times in hunting that staying completely still was the best hiding any animal could ever do. He had had lots of game walk right past him over the years, simply because he didn't move.

Now, he just hoped the Skaarj were no better than wild animals at seeing danger.

His hands gripped the rifle. His every sense seemed to be on extra high intensity.

Every sound seemed loud.

Every breath seemed as if it could be heard for miles.

He would have bet that his heartbeat could be heard ten paces away.

On both sides of him the brush cracking continued. Clearly, they were making no effort to sneak up on anything. Or they simply didn't know how, which Haute figured was more likely.

Sweat dripped off his forehead and down his nose. He ignored it.

Not moving.

Almost not even breathing.

Slowly, the noise moved past him and out into the open fields of the castle.

He took a slow, deep breath and then eased himself silently back up to where he could see from under the tree, making sure his rifle stayed low so that it didn't accidentally catch and reflect sun off its barrel.

The two Skaarj that had passed him in the trees were now twenty paces out into the field and moving slowly toward the castle.

Two other Skaarj had appeared from the trees on the other side of the road and were doing the same thing. Those around the transport waited until the others were abreast of their position, then four of them started forward, leaving two with the transport.

They were clearly well trained and very good at what they did. Their problem was that they were also predictable. And so far, they were acting exactly as the scouts had said they would act.

Two Skaarj stopped at the body of the dead guard at the gate and quickly inspected it. Haute was very tempted to fire at the explosive sticks on the wall over their head, but more than likely the explosion wouldn't take even half of them out. And then he would be in trouble.

The plan was for him to wait, to let them go in and inspect the mine. After Bccui and Rentahs had blown the explosives over the mine, they would retreat to a position to cover him when he detonated the explosives over the front archway as the survivors came out.

Then he, Bccui, and Rentahs would run. That was his plan and no matter how tempting it was right now to change it and blow up the archway, he needed to stay with his plan.

Two by two, the Skaarj moved under the arch and into the market area. Haute could see them through the stone arch as they inspected the dead bodies of the other Skaarj, then moved on toward the mine.

Now, the front of the castle was left to him and the two Skaarj with the transport.

Silence flooded the area as Haute kept his rifle ready. Both Skaarj stood guard near the front of the transport. A good shot at the explosive in the brush just might take both of them out at the same time.

The seconds seemed to stretch as Haute waited. He could imagine the Skaarj moving down the streets toward the mine, moving quickly and surely.

Bccui and Rentahs would wait until they had gathered in front of the mine, or even better, had gone inside, before blowing the hillside. So waiting was all they could do.

All he could do.

Haute made himself breathe slow, deep breaths that calmed him and kept him focused on the Skaarj at the transport and his explosive targets in the brush and on the wall.

Suddenly, the waiting ended.

There were two Skaarj weapons blasts, then an instant of silence.

The hillside above the castle seemed to expand outward like a water bag filled too full.

The ground shook harder than any earthquake Haute had ever felt, as the air around him smashed against the trees fiercer than the worst storm.

And as quickly as it had started, it was past him.

A huge cloud of dust and dirt billowed out over the back of the castle, swallowing the stone towers and walls like a hungry animal eating small game.

Ten of those explosive sticks going off at once made a massive impact. There was no doubt from the size of that explosion that the mine entrance was closed. Haute just hoped about eight Skaarj were trapped under the rubble.

The two Skaarj near the transport started forward toward the castle.

Haute took dead aim on the explosive stick in the bush beside the road. He waited for an instant until they were both even with it, then pulled the trigger and held it down.

The gun kicked slightly in his hand as the blue and green beam pulsed out. At first, he thought he had missed the target.

Then the explosion smashed the two Skaarj into the air, sending one flying head over heels above the transport.

The blast whipped the transport around and rolled it over like a child's toy. A moment later, it burst into flames and exploded.

The Skaarj closest to the blast was torn apart. The biggest piece Haute could see was his torso.

The dust cloud from that explosion floated and swirled in the air for a moment before being blown to Haute's left, opening up his view of the front arch of the castle.

Haute glanced at the Skaarj that had been thrown over the transport. There was no telling if he was still alive, and Haute couldn't take the chance. With a quick shot he hit the Skaarj squarely in the chest, rolling him over and over across the road. If he hadn't been dead before, he was now.

The cloud of billowing dust from the hillside collapse was mostly moving upward and along the hillside. The mass of it wouldn't reach the front arch. So Haute could still see his target there.

Haute aimed the rifle at the three explosive sticks to the right of the archway. If he blew those, the others would explode also, sending up a blast almost as big as the one at the back of the castle. No one within a hundred paces of that archway would live through it.

The echoing thunder from the first two explosions died off into the distant mountains.

Haute didn't move, focusing on his target, forcing himself to breathe long, slow breaths.

Nothing but the dust seemed to be moving inside the castle.

Again, time seemed to go into slow motion around him. Haute forced himself to keep his gaze on the entrance to the castle.

The dust cloud billowed and slowly settled.

Nothing inside moved.

After what seemed like an eternity, a voice behind him said, "Haute?"

"Here," he whispered.

Both Rentahs and Bccui walked up beside him.

He forced himself to look away from the front gate and up at his brother, standing like a fool out in the open.

Bccui was smiling.

So was Rentahs.

"We got them all," Bccui said. "And I see you took care of the two out here."

"All?" Haute asked, not really believing what his brother was telling him. "Are you sure?"

"Completely," Rentahs said. "Eight of them were standing just inside the cave mouth when we blew it."

"That explosion was focused downward," Bccui said, "by the location of the charges. Nothing under it could have survived."

Rentahs laughed. "It almost knocked me down the hillside, and I was a hundred paces above and to the side of the blast. Not right under it."

Bccui nodded. "That stuff is very, very powerful, that's for sure."

"Makes sense," Rentahs said. "They use it to blast solid rock."

Haute let his grip on his rifle relax a little. There was still nothing but dust moving inside the castle walls. Maybe they had gotten them all.

Just maybe.

Bccui and Rentahs were sure talking as if they had. They had no doubts.

Haute stood, realizing for the first time that his legs were shaky and weak.

He pulled out his water bottle and took a long drink, then handed it to his brother, who did the same.

The water felt great as it cleared the dust from his throat and filled him with energy. Enough to realize that they had to finish here and head for home.

He held his rifle at the ready and headed into the open toward the front of the castle. "Come on," he said to the two behind him. "We have some work to finish."

Thirty minutes later, they had checked to make sure the Skaarj really were buried under the side of the mountain, retrieved the explosive sticks from the side of the archway, and got the extra ammunition belts and weapons from the two dead near the burning transport.

Then the three turned and headed into the mountains and their cavern home. All three were happy. Happier than Haute had remembered being since the Skaarj landed. Today they had killed sixteen Skaarj.

There were almost two hundred more, but there were sixteen fewer.

Haute doubted that the rest would be as easy. But for the moment, they could celebrate.

And Haute could laugh with his brother and friend, as long as the image of his own death didn't sneak into his thoughts.

Chapter 12

Second Occupation

Zofia chased everybody but the Nali technician out of
the room before she undressed and stepped into the
fountain. The tech had adjusted the controls so the
shower wouldn't affect her implants—Gerick had
guessed right about that—but she wondered what else
it might do to her. She would soon find out; she was
tired enough of the twinges from her cracked rib and
all her other injuries that she was willing to take the
risk.

The water was pleasant enough all by itself. She
followed Gerick's lead and took the opportunity to
scrub, even though she had bathed in the river that
morning. She had sweated plenty since then.

Somewhere in the middle of her shower, she realized it didn't hurt anymore to raise her left arm or
twist sideways. She didn't hurt anywhere. She felt
better than she had ever felt in her life. It was as if the
fountain was pouring energy directly into her cells,
healing her from the very foundation of her being.

After about five minutes, the tech told her she could come out. She toweled off and dressed in fresh clothing from her pack, an all-black outfit she had found in the chaplain's quarters. With the collar left open, it looked pretty good. It was the first time in a long while that she had really cared.

On a whim, she stuck an extra pair of socks in her shirt, arranging them so they stuck *way* out in front, then she opened the door.

Gerick took one look at her and burst out laughing. Boris merely stared.

"Roll up your tongue," she told him as she pulled out the socks. She wadded one up and threw it at Gerick, who caught it and snapped it at her. She threw the other one at Boris, who caught it and kept it.

"You going to try it?" she asked him, tilting her head toward the fountain.

He shook his head. "Not just yet. Maybe tomorrow, if you don't turn into a rutabaga or something overnight."

"What's the matter?" Gerick asked. "Chicken?"

Boris gave him a sideways frown. "No, just healthy."

Gerick poked him in the stomach. "Yeah, that roll of flab looks healthy to me."

Boris said nothing. Zofia took back her socks and stuck them into her pack, then asked Ranel, "So what's next?"

The Nali leader said, "We should meet with the other resistance advisers and decide where you will be most useful."

"I don't recall actually agreeing to help," Zofia reminded her, but in truth she felt so wonderful she probably would have agreed to take on the entire

Skaarj homeworld if the Nali asked her to. She wondered if that was why they had given her the treatment, so she would feel invincible.

Ranel merely said, "Of course," and led the group out of the hospital and on into the honeycomb of tunnels.

They never made it to wherever she was taking them. They were climbing a set of wide stone stairs when they heard an explosion and screams from above. The ground shook, and dust sifted down out of cracks overhead.

"What was that?" Gerick asked, drawing his automag.

Ranel said, "I don't know, but it didn't sound good."

They raced up the stairs. Another explosion echoed through the tunnels, and they heard more screams. This time, they could make out the words: "Skaarj!"

"They followed us here!" Melnori said.

Ranel whirled around, drawing a matte black pistol with an inchwide barrel as she did so, and aimed it straight at Zofia's head. "Traitors!"

"It wasn't us," Zofia said.

Gerick was right beside Ranel; he held his automag to her head and told her, "Put the gun down."

Ranel didn't flinch, and she didn't remove her gun from Zofia's head. "You put yours down," she said.

More explosions came from above. The clamor of a heated gun battle grew louder. Boris stepped up the stairs behind Zofia.

"Stop!" Ranel glanced toward him, but her pistol never wavered from Zofia's face.

Boris said, "You're not going to shoot anybody until you know for sure what happened. In the meantime, we're all in danger. While you're sorting all this out, I'm going to go kill some Skaarj." He kept climbing the stairs.

"Don't go alone!" Zofia said, but he disappeared around the corner. She looked Ranel straight in the eye and said, "He's going to get himself killed if we don't help him."

Ranel obviously didn't know what to do. Gunshots and screams echoed in the tunnels. She looked to Melnori, then back at Zofia, then she finally lowered her pistol. "Go, then. But I will be right behind you. At the first sign of betrayal, all three of you will die."

"Fair enough." Zofia stepped past her, taking her tarydium stinger and her flak gun from their holsters and making sure they were loaded and ready to go. The scale on the side of the stinger had a green dot about a third of the way down; there were still plenty of shots left.

Melnori reached into a fold in his pants and took out a tiny pistol—obviously something the humans had overlooked when they had captured him. Zofia shook her head and handed him the laser, which she had been carrying in her pack. "Unless that thing's more powerful than it looks, you're better off with this," she said.

He took it from her gratefully. "Thank you."

She ran to the top of the stairs and turned toward the source of the noise. She could see Boris a hundred feet ahead, just disappearing around a curve in the tunnel. "Wait up!" she shouted, but he didn't stop.

Gerick ran alongside her, his automag in his left hand and his fragger in his right. For once, Zofia was glad for his company. They rushed around the corner after Boris, and she nearly screamed at the sight that awaited her.

The passage opened out into another large cavern. Just like at the arsenal, stalactites hung down from the ceiling like long icicles tipped with bright sunglobes, but instead of weapons, this one contained the wreckage of electronic equipment, and the floor was covered with dead and dying bodies.

Most of them were Nali. A dozen Skaarj lay among the dead, and Zofia even spotted a few aliens of other races, but it was clear who was losing this battle. It wasn't for lack of trying—Nali fighters rushed out of all the side passages like water out of firehoses, but the Skaarj just mowed them down as fast as they appeared. There were twenty or thirty of the big green monsters about two-thirds of the way across the cavern, and they were using some kind of plasma weapons they didn't even have to aim; they just swept the room with them, and the beams of energy automatically jumped like lightning bolts from person to person, frying them on the spot.

And Boris stood right out there in plain sight, firing his flak gun at them like a kid plinking at cans. Only the distance between the Skaarj and the rear entrance to the cavern had spared him so far.

The noise was deafening. Every shot echoed, and everyone was either yelling orders or screaming in agony. Zofia didn't even try to coordinate with anybody; she just fired tarydium crystals into the thickest knot of Skaarj, hitting two of them before she triggered the blast with her flak gun. There were five or six in the group, but she never got a better count than that before the two she'd hit exploded like bombs, taking the others with them and throwing body parts clear across the cavern.

That drew the others' attention, though. Bright energy bolts lanced out toward her from a dozen different sources, and she jumped for cover behind a big metal cabinet. Sparks erupted all around her, showering against the stone wall, but the cabinet grounded the charge long enough for her to run for cover behind another one. The brilliant discharge had apparently hid her from the Skaarj; they didn't fire at her new hiding place. She peeked over the edge just long enough to spot another two of them together over on the right side of the cavern, then fired slivers of tarydium into them.

Boris saw the glow and detonated them before she had a chance to fire her own fragger at them.

"Take cover, you idiot!" she shouted at him, but with all the shouts and screams echoing in the cavern, he didn't hear her.

Gerick had gone left when Zofia went right; under cover of the Nali crossfire, he worked his way toward Boris, ducking behind desks and cabinets until he got close enough to pull him down behind an overturned table. She could hear them shouting at each other, but the Skaarj sprayed plasma all around her again, and she couldn't tell what they were saying.

Melnori and Ranel had taken cover in an alcove just to the right of the door, and were leaning out and taking pot shots every few seconds. Zofia worked her way back toward them, and when she was within earshot she shouted, "Where are your gun emplacements?"

"Our what?" Ranel shouted back.

"Gun emplacements! Big guns mounted up high so you can cover the whole cavern."

Ranel's blank look told her everything she needed

to know. "You didn't provide for defense in your own stronghold?"

"Not here. This is the command center!"

Right. If the enemy had made it this far, the war was already lost. Well the enemy was here, but Zofia wasn't giving up just yet. There were only a dozen or so Skaarj left, and they had taken cover, too.

If Zofia couldn't climb up to a better vantage point, then she needed to get closer. "Cover me!" she shouted, then because she didn't know if the Nali understood the concept, she said, "That means keep shooting so they keep their heads down."

They obliged, and Zofia was glad to see that Ranel's gun at least provided flash and sound to match its bore. Melnori fired bright beams of laser light out through the smoke and dust in the air. Dozens of other Nali were firing dozens of different weapons, too; the air was thick with bright flashes and energy beams.

It was getting hard to see through all the smoke. Zofia ran forward until she was abreast of Gerick and Boris, maybe twenty feet to the right, and fired her stinger at the source of one of the plasma bolts before ducking behind a computer console. The tarydium crystal spattered off the floor in front of the desk the Skaarj was hiding behind, but the explosion merely blew a crater in the rock and sent shards flying.

The concussion also knocked a stalactite free. It smashed down right behind the same Skaarj, and he leaped for safety.

Boris jumped up and fired at him, catching him in the shoulder and spinning him around. He kept firing his fragger, *boom, boom, boom,* determined to kill the Skaarj before he could take cover again, but an energy bolt lanced out from behind a wall divider and caught him square in the chest.

"Boris!" Zofia screamed. She leaped up and ran for him, ducking another plasma bolt as it veered toward her like something alive. She fired the stinger sideways as she ducked, and was gratified to hear a Skaarj scream in agony an instant before another explosion rocked the cavern.

She dropped down beside Boris, who lay on his back behind the upturned conference table with a smoking hole in his chest.

"No!" she yelled. "Don't you die on me, damn it. Not now."

His eyes fluttered open. "That's . . . what *she* said," he whispered. He even tried to sit up, but she pushed him back down.

"Stay there, you stupid bastard. You think they can't hit you twice?"

He laughed, but it turned into a cough. When he got it under control again, he said, "I didn't think . . . they could hit me once. Mistake."

"You're damned right it was a mistake. Gerick, drag him back—Gerick?"

He had disappeared. Zofia looked toward the back of the room, expecting to see him retreating, but then she heard the distinctive *boom* of a flak gun in the other direction. She looked over the edge of the table and saw him advancing steadily on the Skaarj, jumping from cover to cover with each shot.

A fine time for him to get brave. It had to be the effect of the fountain. "Come back here!" she yelled at him, but he either didn't hear her or just ignored her.

"Stay put," she told Boris, then she darted out from

behind the table, firing both flak gun and stinger as she ran after Gerick.

A plasma bolt grazed her side before she could dodge it. Her breath left her in one convulsive scream, and she fell to the rock floor, but she turned the fall into a roll and slammed into the back of a desk. She thanked her luck that the Nali liked metal furniture; the plasma bolt sprayed outward, scintillating like fireworks all around her.

She heard another *boom,* this time from behind her. She turned her head to see Boris up again and firing over the edge of the table.

The plasma bolt zigzagged away from her, straight at Boris.

"Duck!" she yelled, and he was already trying to, but it was too late. The energy beam struck him in the head with a bright flash before it winked out.

"No!" Zofia rushed back to him, leaping over the table and nearly landing on his chest, but she twisted in midair and missed him. She bent down to look at his face and nearly gagged at the sight; his left cheek had been burned down to the bone, and what flesh was left below his eye had been cooked until it smoked.

The right side and the top of his head looked almost normal. "Boris, talk to me," Zofia said to him. "Damn it, Boris, don't die on me. Boris!" She felt for a pulse in his neck, and at first she didn't find it, but then her thumb jiggled ever so slightly.

She had to get him to the healing fountain. She stood up to drag him away, but a plasma bolt instantly reached out for her, and she had to drop back down. She would never make it to the door.

Gerick was still firing away up ahead. He couldn't

have much more ammunition. In a moment she would have two wounded friends if she didn't do something.

The Skaarj knew where she was. Plasma bolts flashed out and scintillated off the table, heating it cherry red. They didn't stay in one place long enough to burn through, though, and suddenly Zofia realized what Gerick was doing. He was protecting her. Buying her time.

She couldn't even peek over the tabletop to shoot, and she was afraid to shoot blind for fear of hitting Gerick. Time was rapidly running out. Zofia did the only thing she could think of: she aimed at the cavern ceiling above the Skaarj and fired her stinger again and again.

Tarydium crystals exploded on impact with the hard rock, blasting stalactites loose to rain down like arrows on the Skaarj. She heard their agonized screams, and the plasma beams winked out one by one.

The gun ran out after twenty or thirty more shots, but she had done the job. The cavern echoed with the last of the falling debris, then an eerie calm settled over it as the defenders realized no more Skaarj were firing.

Zofia grabbed Boris by the arms and hauled him toward the door. Melnori and Ranel met her there and helped her rush him to the hospital, where they elbowed their way past the dozens of other people already there and pushed their way right past the examination room techs to a healing room.

"Make way!" Melnori shouted. "Critical wounds!"

The door opened and the same tech who had run the fountain for Gerick and Zofia looked out. The

moment he saw Boris he backed away and let them
bring him in, helping the Nali patient who was in the
water to hobble out—his chest still partly singed from
a similar plasma wound—to wait on the bench.
Melnori helped Zofia hold Boris under the fountain's
gentle spray, but after only a few seconds his head
lolled forward and his whole body went slack.

"Live, damn it," Zofia said. "Live!" But it was clear
he was beyond hearing her.

"I'm sorry, but he's gone." The tech reached out to
help her carry him out, but she backed farther into the
fountain with him.

"Get back! Give him a chance."

The tech waited a few more seconds, then said,
"He's dead, and there are other patients who need the
fountain."

Zofia looked past him out the doorway. Wounded
Nali were streaming into the hospital by the hundreds. She caught a glimpse of Gerick among them,
his entire right side scorched black, before the crowd
closed up around him.

She lifted Boris's head. "Come on, buddy. Wake up.
Wake up *now.*"

No response. Running water plastered his hair
down over his forehead. She couldn't look at the rest
of his face.

Melnori stepped out of the fountain, gently pulling
her along with him. She let him lead her away, both of
them supporting Boris, whose legs dragged over the
lip of the pool and out the door. He felt twice as heavy
now as he had just a moment ago. They carried him
over to a corner and lay him down beside a Nali
corpse in even worse shape than he was. Zofia leaned
against the wall and tilted her head back, closing her
eyes. *Don't cry,* she told herself. *Don't cry.*

It was useless. She was glad she was already soaking wet.

She realized that her shirt clung to her chest more loosely than it should. They hadn't programmed the fountain this time. She wasn't surprised to realize that she didn't care.

"He fought bravely," Melnori said. His voice sounded flat, unemotional.

She opened her eyes and looked over at him. He stood there with all four arms hanging limp, the laser rifle dangling by its strap, forgotten.

She looked beyond him at the other Nali, crowding into the hospital like sheep in a corner of a pen after the wolf has been through. Stunned, every one of them, at what they had just witnessed.

But not fired up for revenge. Zofia couldn't see that in a single one of them, not even Melnori or Ranel.

"Wake up, damn it!" she shouted, but this time she wasn't shouting at Boris. "All of you, wake up! They're going to come back." Heads turned toward her. A sea of alien faces fixed on her. "Look," she told them, "it's now or never. It's time to get up off your sorry asses and take back your planet! You've got maybe half an hour before the Skaarj move in here with everything they've got—you can either clear out now with what weapons you can carry, or you can wait for them to come wipe out your last hope. Which will it be?"

Nobody answered. Zofia looked down at Boris's body, then back out at the Nali. She swallowed, then shouted, "I say let's kill the fuckers. Let's kill every last one of 'em, and send their heads home in a box!"

A low murmur rose in the crowd. A few voices shouted something in the native tongue, then Gerick's voice cut through them like a knife. "Death to the Skaarj!" Zofia didn't know who was more surprised, she or the Nali, but he said it again, "Death to the Skaarj!" and this time a few more voices joined his. Zofia added hers the third time around, and they kept shouting. More and more picked it up, louder and louder, until the entire mountain seemed to ring with their voices.

Chapter 13

First Occupation

The small fire gave the cave they called the council chamber a warm, almost cozy feel. Haute glanced around at the others sitting comfortably around the flames. Bccui, his brother, rested against a small stump at Haute's left. Ablee and Jeeie both sat on rocks, both sipping cups of fresh root tea Ablee had brewed. Targee's large bulk rested against the rock wall.

The fire had heated the air in the small cavern to a warm, almost toasty level. And after the great dinner of fish and fresh vegetables Ablee and his kitchen crew had prepared, Haute felt more like sleeping than meeting and planning. But planning was important, especially now that they had really hit the Skaarj hard.

Because of their attack, Haute was convinced that things had changed. He was also convinced that over the next few months the situation would continue to change. If Jeeie's scouting information about the

Skaarj was correct, they wouldn't much like the fact that the Mountain Fighters had beaten them.

Haute leaned back against a log and let his legs stretch out in front of him on the rock floor, focusing his mind off the idea of sleep. His legs and body were still very, very sore from the long, fast hike they had made back from the castle attack. It had taken two days of climbing, backtracking, and wading streams to get here, making completely sure that the Skaarj couldn't track them. He'd been home for a day now, and his legs still ached.

He took a long sip of Ablee's tea and tried to focus his mind on the next attack against the Skaarj, instead of on the soothing orange flicker of the fire. He and Ablee had talked privately about Haute's visions of two more attacks on castles. Both of them agreed that was the best line of offense, if none of the others had major objections.

"Jeeie," Ablee said in the group around the fire, moving to get the talking started for the night, "have you gotten a complete count of what supplies we got from the last attack?"

Jeeie was in charge of the day-to-day operations of the more than two hundred cavern residents, including fishing and hunting parties, weapons and ammunition stock, and sleeping quarters. He was very, very good at his job, never seeming to miss a chance to increase the food supplies, or to put the Nali to work at something they were good at.

"A good haul," Jeeie said in response to Ablee's question. "Sixteen extra working Skaarj rifles, with twenty full ammunition belts holding over four hundred charges."

"Great," Haute said. He hadn't realized, mostly because of his headache, that the searchers of the

Skaarj quarters near the mine had found so many weapons.

"Now, we just need to find Nali who aren't afraid to fire them at Skaarj," Ablee said.

No one around the fire said a word to that. It was the biggest problem they had. Only about one in five Nali was capable of fighting. There was just something about the Nali makeup that made them complete pacifists. At the moment, with the new weapons, they had more guns than they had Nali who could use them against Skaarj.

"We also retrieved almost two full cases of mining explosives," Jeeie said.

"How many sticks is that?" Bccui asked.

"Just under two hundred," Jeeie said.

Targee whistled softly.

"Stored away from the caverns, I hope," Haute said. He had been completely surprised at how powerful each of those sticks was. Two hundred of them going off at once would be enough to almost level a mountain.

"Way away," Jeeie said, grinning. "I heard the stories of how powerful that stuff is. It's stored in a small cave over the ridge from here."

"How many of us are trained to fight?" Ablee asked, turning to Targee. Targee and Bccui were in charge of training those who were able to fight. After seeing young Rentahs at work, Haute knew the training was topnotch.

"About fifty," Targee said.

Bccui nodded his agreement.

Ablee seemed to make a mental note of the number. "And how many of those does it take to guard the caverns?"

"Sixteen," Jeeie said and this time it was Targee who nodded his agreement.

"So there're thirty-four fighters available for the next attack against the Skaarj," Haute said.

"Give or take a few," Bccui said.

Thirty-four against at least two hundred trained Skaarj fighters. Haute didn't like the odds, but they were a lot better than they had been when the Skaarj ship first crashed. Then, it was two hundred Skaarj against a society that had never learned to fight. Thus, there had been no fight.

The fire crackled, but no one spoke. Haute waited, sipping his tea, letting the warm liquid flow down his throat and ease the tension the conversation was bringing up.

"So," Ablee said into the silence. "Where or what do we hit next?"

No one said a word, so with only a glance at Ablee, Haute said, "Notsiwel and Wocsom." Both were castles just north of the one they had just taken. Still far south of the main body of Skaarj, and still a long distance from the caverns. Both were guarded by small numbers of Skaarj.

"Which one first?" Bccui asked, nodding at the choices.

Haute shook his head. "No, both at the same time, on the same day. And we don't stop there."

Even Targee leaned forward, his normally calm face puzzled by Haute's words.

"Why?" Ablee asked.

"Simple," Haute said. "We need to draw a line behind which our people will be safe. And then we defend the line."

Ablee stared at Haute for a moment, then smiled as Haute's idea slowly became clear to him.

"Let me get this straight," Ablee said, grabbing a few loose rocks. He placed one near his foot on a smooth area of the cave floor, then another stone about three inches away, and a third about two inches from that. Then he put a fourth stone seven or eight inches away from the third, all almost in a line. Then using his finger, he drew a faint line in the dust on the floor between the stones.

"Castles Notsiwel and Wocsom," he said, pointing at the two middle stones and looking at Haute.

Haute nodded.

Ablee pointed at the fourth stone, the farthest from the two central ones. "Castle Tniopdnas to the north. Right?"

"Correct," Haute said, smiling at his friend. "What's between Tniopdnas and Wocsom?"

Ablee drew a line directly down the middle of the area between the two stones.

"The Edacsac Mountains," Bccui said.

"And Rennod Pass," Jeeie said.

Haute nodded. "Hard to travel, easy to defend. We clean out the Skaarj south of that pass and we have a defensible position."

Ablee nodded, then glanced at Haute. "You have an idea about just how we can clean out the Skaarj south of there?"

"I do," Haute said. And for the next two hours he explained it.

And for the next two days they planned it.

Six days after returning to the caverns, Haute left them again, knowing deep inside that he would never return.

The second castle vision came true on the third day after leaving the caverns. Haute found himself at sunrise, staring down at the castle Wocsom. Normally, he would have found the castle beautiful, with the trees growing around it and the open meadow in front. But this cold morning he wasn't looking at the beauty of the setting, only at the ugliness of having Skaarj inside the castle.

Young Rentahs stood beside him, Skaarj rifle at the ready. Scattered through the trees were four other Nali, all good fighters as far as Haute could tell. Only six of them to take a castle. He hoped it could be done.

Bccui led a group of ten fighters to the south of Wocsom, ready to take the castle Notsiwel. They had decided that would be the first line of attack. Jeeie's scouts had told them that during the last attack, the Skaarj had sent reinforcements from the nearest castle, leaving only two Skaarj to guard it until a transport of Skaarj could come in from the north.

Haute's plan counted on them doing the same thing if castle Notsiwel was attacked. Skaarj reinforcements would leave here and move south. Along the way, Targee and six others would stop them before they ever reached the castle, blowing them up on the road with hidden explosive sticks.

To the north, another team of Mountain Fighters were set up on the pass to block any reinforcements coming in from there. If this plan worked, within a few hours there wouldn't be a Skaarj left alive south of the Edacsac Mountains.

"Almost time," Rentahs said, moving back slightly as the sun peaked above the tops of the mountains. That would be Bccui's team's signal to start.

Haute also moved back and crouched as the light brightened over the meadow between him and the castle. He was close enough here to feel just the faint start of a headache. Nothing bad, yet. But enough to remind him how bad it was going to get.

In the distance, the faint sound of thunder. Only there wasn't a storm cloud in the air. That was the sound of Bccui's team starting the attack on the castle.

Haute glanced at Rentahs. "Pass the word to get ready and move into positions. It's started."

Rentahs silently moved back into the deeper trees. Haute checked the charges in his rifle, then made sure that he had ten sticks of explosive in his pockets. With the explosive, he was like a walking bomb. If a Skaarj shot hit him, there wouldn't be a piece of his body left big enough to pick up and bury.

Rentahs appeared silently back at his side, just as a rumble from inside the castle echoed over the valley.

"Transport," Haute whispered. "Right on time."

A moment later a Skaarj transport appeared under the castle's main archway and bounced down the road, going as fast as the rough road would allow it to move. There was a driver, and four Skaarj were in the back. The scouts had said there were seven Skaarj in this castle, so that left two guarding it, just as Haute had planned.

The transport disappeared into the trees. A moment later another faint rumble of an explosion filled the air. Bccui's team was at full assault. Haute hoped it was going smoothly. Targee's team would intercept the transport about three miles down the road.

"Let's go," Haute said.

With Rentahs behind him, the two of them moved down to the left side of the castle, working their way through the trees for cover until they were within thirty paces of the stone walls. The Skaarj guard would be stationed right around the left side of the archway. And unlike the last time, Haute wasn't going to just walk out and shout. He had no doubt that he would be killed instantly.

This time he planned on using young Rentahs' shooting ability to take out the guard.

"Ready?" Haute whispered, glancing around at Rentahs.

The young fighter nodded and brought his rifle up into firing position, aiming it at the archway.

Haute pulled out one explosive stick and held it gently in one hand.

"Here we go," he said. With a long, flowing underhand motion that he had practiced for two hours a few days before, he tossed the explosive stick at the gate.

Rentahs followed the high arch of the stick with his rifle and then, just as the stick was about to hit the ground inside the archway, and right in front of where the Skaarj guard would be posted, he fired.

The beam caught the stick perfectly.

The blast sent them both backward into the brush and filled the main archway of the castle with dust and smoke.

Instantly, Haute rolled and came back to his feet, weapon ready.

A moment later Rentahs did the same, a cut bleeding just above his hairline on his forehead.

Haute ran for the wall, moving along it for cover until he reached the archway. Then, staying down low, he moved inside and to the left, toward the Skaarj guard station.

From the back of the castle near the mine entrance came the sounds of Skaarj rifle fire. Two quick blasts, followed by a third, then silence.

Haute waited against the stone wall, breathing in

the dust and smoke of the explosion until Rentahs reached a position on the right of the archway. A position that could cover Haute if the Skaarj guard had managed to survive that explosion.

Rentahs nodded when he was in position.

Haute took a deep breath and moved quickly toward the open Skaarj guard station. The moment he could see inside he knew the explosion had worked. The Skaarj had been smashed against the back stone wall. It looked to Haute as if every bone in its body had been smashed by the force of the concussion in the small stone room. It had worked exactly as he had hoped.

One of the other Mountain Fighters was carefully working his way down the main boulevard, headed toward the market area to back up Haute and Rentahs just in case they needed it. Rentahs was supposed to do the same thing in case those near the mine needed help. So it seemed they had taken the castle.

The second castle in eight days.

From a distance, the sounds of another explosion drifted over the trees and meadow. More than likely it was Targee's group ambushing the transport.

Haute stopped and, just for a moment, listened to the sounds of war.

Chapter 14

Second Occupation

Zofia watched the attack on the landing craft's six-inch control monitor. It was a cramped proposition; the copilot's chair was made for a birdlike alien about half her height. The pilot's chair was no more spacious; besides, it was occupied by the lander's original owner, a muscle-bound white-and-silver hawk with an oversized head and clawed fingers at the ends of his wings. He went by the name of Quoin, as near as she could make out, and he was very possessive about his spaceship.

Zofia didn't blame him. This was probably the only spaceworthy craft on Na Pali that didn't belong to the Skaarj. Too bad it could only go into orbit and back, but that was still better than most other ships that came here.

The lander had been in the cargo hold of Quoin's starship, which hadn't been designed to land, and unfortunately hadn't been designed to withstand the disruptive effects of a planet-sized mass of tarydium, either. Quoin and the landing craft had been the only survivors.

He had spent the three years since his arrival shielding its electronic systems from tarydium interference and mounting weapons on it. Now, he was itching to try it out on the Skaarj, but Melnori had persuaded him to wait until after dark to attack.

He didn't like that, but Melnori had a good point: most of the other aircraft would be hampered at night by their lack of instrumentation. It made sense to save the lander for the time when its radar and infrared sensors would give it the best advantage.

Zofia didn't like waiting, either. Quoin had tapped into the Skaarj communication satellites so they could watch the battle unfold, but she felt guilty watching other people fight and die when she was safe on the ground a hundred miles away.

"We need to get inside the city," she said to Melnori, who crouched behind her chair. Gerick sat cross-legged behind him, cleaning his fragger and his automag. Ranel had gone off with another group of fighters so the resistance wouldn't lose two leaders if the lander was shot down. "If we just blow it up from outside, it won't do you guys any good. We have to capture it and hold it, the more intact the better, so we can use its weapons against the other cities."

"That's another reason to wait," Melnori said. "We don't want to be in Rrajigar while it's under attack. Let our fighters soften them up first, take out some of their guns and spread chaos throughout the city; then we can sneak in and do what we can from inside."

Gerick racked the action back and forth on his automag. "How are we going to get in, hot shot? From what I can see on that video-wristwatch there, it looks to me like they've got perimeter defenses half a mile out."

"Easily avoided," Quoin said. His voice was soft, but clear. "I can put you down right at the base of the cliff."

"Which leaves us with a defended mesa to climb."

"Perhaps not," Melnori said. He pointed at a billowing cloud of smoke at one edge of the city. "See there; the power station has been hit. That means the cooling water is probably not flowing any more. The pipes are as wide as a Nali is tall; we could go in through them."

"Inside the pipes?" Zofia asked. "What about footing? What about the pumps?"

"The pumps won't be running. And the pipes will be full of slessums. They're a kind of shellfish that sticks to piers and rocks and things. They'll provide all the traction we need."

"Huh. Well, nobody will be looking for us there, that's for sure."

Melnori said, "In the meantime, I have something else I want to investigate. There's a chance we can do better than the pipes."

"Oh?"

"It's something Ranel told me about before I woke you to introduce her to you, but we didn't have a chance to discuss it later."

Zofia looked back at him. "What?"

"Quoin, back the view out until we have the entire mountain range in the screen." When the hawk-creature did that, Melnori reached past Zofia and tapped the screen at a spot to the southeast of where they were. "Expand this section. Good, now expand again on this. And here. And again here. What do you see?"

"I see a bunch of rock and bushes," said Zofia.

"I see fourteen small burrowing animals and a lizard," said Quoin.

"Precisely," said Melnori. "Now, take us there."

"That's easy enough." Quoin touched the controls and the lander rose soundlessly on its repulsors, then raced away to the south. Within minutes, he had slowed down again and was about to land, but the collision alarm went off when they were still fifty feet up.

"What? There's nothing here."

"No?" asked Melnori. "Move over aways and set down. Gently; I don't know the extent of it myself."

"The extent of what?"

The lander settled on the ground, and Melnori led the four occupants to the airlock. "Three days ago, observers saw a ship come in under power. From the time and the path described to me, I think it was the one I believe we saw that first night at Tien Camp. It landed here—and disappeared."

Zofia looked out the airlock at the reddish rocks and greenish-yellow scrub-brush. Now that she knew what to look for, she could see a faint outline of shimmering fuzziness, most apparent against the smooth orange sky of sunset. Something big and oblong in shape rested there, but it was projecting the image from directly behind it, no matter what angle you looked from.

"Whose is it?" she asked.

"We don't know. Our advance scouts never returned."

Gerick cocked his flak gun loudly. "Now you tell us."

Melnori shrugged. "A Skaarj force investigated it not long after our scouts arrived. There were four of them. Three left a few hours later. We can assume that one was killed in a battle with the ship's crew, and that the other three killed the crew in turn."

"Or one is still here, standing guard."

"Unlikely. Anyone who was here would have been recalled to defend Rrajigar by now."

"That's why you had us wait," said Zofia.

"Yes. Now, let us go see if this ship will help us in any way."

They walked toward it, weapons drawn. The illusion persisted until they were nearly upon it; then within the last twenty feet or so the pixels grew large enough so that the image became obviously fake, and within ten feet the structure of the ship became apparent.

"There's the airlock," Quoin said, pointing with a wing.

It was big enough for a human to stand in comfortably. The cycle button was at just the right height, with red and green indicator lights above it. Zofia pushed the button and the green one lit up. A moment later the door slid aside, revealing a rectangular airlock. Pressure suits hung from a rack on one side; safety lines and harnesses were stored on the other. Zofia had seen suits and airlocks like this every day since she was a little girl.

"This is a human ship," she said. She looked up and down its length. The shape looked familiar. It took her a second to remember where she had seen it before, but when it came to her, she felt a chill run down her spine. "Gerick, this is the S–38."

He laughed softly. "So it is."

"What is an S–38?" asked Melnori.

"It's the ship we were stealing the plans for when we were arrested," Zofia explained. "It's why we were sentenced to prison on Kira, which was why we wound up here."

"Too bad we didn't have a chance to actually look at the plans before we got caught," Gerick said.

"We didn't?" Zofia asked. "Maybe you didn't, but I had to make sure we were downloading the right ones." She stepped into the airlock, and the others crowded in with her. She pushed the cycle button, and as the outer door closed and the inner door opened, she said, "There's a central access corridor that runs the whole length of the ship, and there're gun emplacements at 120-degree intervals around the body, both fore and aft. The belly is one big bomb bay, and the armory takes up most of deck two in the aft section."

Gerick said, "That's where we want to go. We need hand weapons and body armor for tonight."

Zofia nodded. "You go for the armory. I want to take a look at the control room. If this thing still flies, we may not need hand weapons. Set on automatic, the waist guns could take out every rooftop defender in Rrajigar in about ten seconds."

Quoin said, "Is it wise to split up? This ship may still be inhabited."

Zofia drew her flak gun from its holster. "I'll be careful."

Before anyone could protest further, she walked away down the hallway that led to the middle of the ship, then turned left and headed forward. The access corridor was brightly lit, and doors led off to either side, but she didn't pause to look behind them. She already knew they were crew quarters.

It wasn't a huge ship. The control room was only a hundred feet or so from the airlock. Zofia palmed the doors open, standing aside just in case somebody *was* inside, but she heard nothing except the soft hum of electronic equipment. She smelled smoke, though, and peered around the door frame and saw that someone had been here. Her heart fell. Most of the control panels had been destroyed by plasma blasts. There were three pools of blood on the floor where bodies had once lain. It had happened quite a while ago; the blood had darkened almost to black. Zofia was glad there weren't any flies on board.

She stepped around the stains and examined the controls. Flight capability was completely destroyed. Fire control likewise. Stealth control still functioned, but she already knew that. The Skaarj had probably left that on purpose, so they could study it.

A monitor set into the control panel at the right of the stealth controls was blinking a message. She bent down to read it, and was surprised to find her own name: *Subject Zofia Mozelle: signal lost 10:23 p.m.* Above that was a similar message: *Subject Gerick Flynn: signal lost 10:18 p.m.* Below was *Subject Boris Liang: signal lost 10:46 p.m.*

She had no idea what internal clock the ship used, but those time stamps had to be the moments when Gerick, then she, then Boris had been in the Nali healing fountain. Foreign objects were dissolved unless the fountain was programmed to keep them; there must have been tracking devices implanted in their bodies.

That alone wasn't surprising. They were prisoners, after all. But why send a stealth warship after them? They weren't that important, were they?

There were four more names. Someone named Sandy Schofield had died at 8:22 a.m. this morning. Not "signal lost," but "deceased." Three more names that Zofia didn't recognize were still listed as alive.

She tapped one of the names, and a menu of choices popped up. She picked "visual" and the screen switched to an overhead view of Rrajigar at twilight. An arrow pointed to one of four towers. The fifth one had collapsed, so this was a real-time image.

The other two names were shown in the same place. Zofia was willing to bet they were the prisoners the Skaarj had taken off the *Rikers* that first night.

She sat down at the monitor and chose her own name, then picked "vital stats" from the list.

Page after page of information scrolled upward. She skimmed over it, astonished at how detailed it was. It mentioned the time she had been arrested when a girlfriend had hidden stolen music in her bag, the time she had tried to ditch the police after her boyfriend had robbed an autobank, and dozens more details out of her past. It documented the break-in at Inuit, but didn't answer the burning question: did she kill any guards or not? On that subject the bio merely said, "Denies killing, evidence inconclusive."

Near the bottom she found a mysterious line: "Committed 10/14/23 to Project Na Pali."

That was a week *before* she'd been shipped out to Kira. Or supposedly to Kira. Apparently, she had been sent here on purpose.

"Na Pali" was flagged as a hot button, but when she tapped it, she got a message that said, "Restricted access. Enter password."

She knew only one: the password that had let her download the ship plans in the first place. She tried that, not really expecting it to work, and it didn't. But when she tried it backward, the screen cleared and she got pages more information.

She didn't have to read far to get the gist of it. Project Na Pali was an experiment to see how well human fighters would fare against the Skaarj. Phase one, of which Zofia was a part, was simple and cheap: strand some bad-ass convicts on the planet near a Skaarj stronghold, give them easy access to military armament, and see how long they lasted.

Phase two would be determined based on phase one's degree of success. If the convicts defeated a fair number of Skaarj before being killed, then ground troops would be used to take the planet. If not, then S–38 stealth fighters would be employed. That would cost more, both in direct expense and in damage to the mining infrastructure that Inuit Corporation would rather keep intact, but they were prepared to pay that price if necessary.

"Those sons of bitches," Zofia muttered. They weren't interested in liberating the Nali. They wanted to perpetuate the same system the Skaarj had established, just redirect the profits, instead.

Her mind reeled with the implications. She'd known she was a pawn in a bigger game when she'd taken the break-in job, but she'd had no idea how little a pawn, or how big the game. And a fresh look at her rap sheet reminded her that this wasn't the first time she'd played the pawn, either. That very first arrest, she hadn't even known she was carrying stolen goods until the mall cops had nailed her. She hadn't known Brian had just robbed an autobank when he'd called her for a ride, either. She hadn't known who had hired her to break into Inuit, or why.

It had probably been Inuit themselves. She looked like a violent criminal on paper, good fodder for their project. They had just needed to lure her into their clutches . . .

She blanked out the screen and stood up. Her head seemed awash with roaring surf. She could almost feel the new information rushing for new homes in her brain, changing everything she had known, everything she had thought about herself. She had to look away, toward somewhere else, anywhere else but that damning monitor.

The FTL radio had not been destroyed. She flipped it on, scanned for traffic. Heard voices.

It would be so simple to call for help. Someone would come, take her off this damned planet. She could warn them about the tarydium interference, and they could land on manual. The war between the Nali and Skaarj would provide excellent cover; they probably wouldn't even be noticed.

And they would almost certainly be from Inuit.

No, calling for help would only play into their hands. They had miscalculated and lost this ship to the Skaarj; now, they had no way to tell how their plan was going. No matter who answered, if she called for help, they would know.

And if she helped the Nali take Rrajigar? Wouldn't they suspect something then?

She didn't know. The Nali had been planning to revolt for years. If Inuit Corporation knew that, they might think the human arrival had merely acted as a catalyst. They would have no reason to think otherwise. Why would escaped convicts join an alien revolution?

Zofia nearly laughed. Because they each thought they might be the Avenging Angel. She had actually bought that line of crap. Not consciously, but every time she had played the hero, that thought had been in the back of her mind. She'd been played for a pawn again, this time by an alien. She hadn't really believed any of his hokey prophecy, but he had managed to manipulate her into thinking she might be able to fulfill it anyway. She'd done what she'd done for other reasons, but the idea had been in the back of her mind from the moment he had told her about it, the notion that she might *become* the avenging angel if she were in the right place at the right time. Might finally become worthwhile to somebody, somewhere.

What a laugh. Ambition makes fools of us all, she thought. She had never amounted to anything in her life; had she really thought she could become the savior of an entire world?

No, she realized. When she put the question that way, it was obvious she hadn't really thought so. She'd never had that strong a self-image. She'd been fooling herself, too.

So what was real? The one honest emotion was the bond she had felt growing between her and Boris. She wanted to avenge his death. That had nothing to do with Inuit Corporation or the Nali. That was all Zofia.

And beyond that?

She looked at the radio. Her link with the rest of humanity. With her past.

She raised the flak gun and fired directly into the panel.

Chapter 15

First Occupation

Haute, with Rentahs right behind him, went through the main archway and ducked left along the remains of the stores and booths that had once lined the busy market center. The smoke from the explosions made his eyes sting, and he could feel his tarydium sensitivity starting to kick in as the throbbing in the back of his head increased.

Targee and five others went to the right after entering the archway, while Bccui and the others followed Haute.

As he passed each booth, each doorway, he checked for Skaarj traps. Nothing but a few Skaarj bodies, smashed almost to a pulp by the contained blast of the explosive sticks, their bodies smelling of acid and tarydium dust, a smell Haute had come to hate as a child. He didn't like it any more, now.

The Mountain Fighters spread themselves through the market area of the castle, facing the three roads leading toward the mine. Haute held up two sticks of explosive so the others could see. Then he wrapped them in twine to hold them together, the same way he had done with the two before.

Targee and Bccui both did the same. Each of them would throw the sticks as far as they could up the streets, then they'd duck for cover as their firing partners set them off.

"Everyone take cover and get ready!" Haute shouted to the others, raising his sticks above his head. His voice echoed through the seemingly empty castle.

Targee and Bccui did the same to indicate that they also were ready.

Rentahs and two other fighters aimed their rifles up the streets, also ready.

"Now!" Haute shouted as he threw the two explosive sticks as far as he could up the main boulevard of the castle.

Targee threw his up the left street.

Bccui threw his up the right.

Just as the sticks Haute had thrown hit the pavement, Rentahs caught them with a perfect shot.

At the same moment, the other shooters hit their targets.

Haute managed to duck around behind a stone edge of a shop door, but the force of six explosive sticks going off at once inside the castle banged him against the wall and almost knocked the air out of him. He sure hoped everyone had found cover.

Rentahs had been tossed by the blast into the room in front of Haute. He climbed to his feet beside Haute, his rifle aimed ahead, as if the blast hadn't even happened. There was no doubt, the young fighter was tough.

A massive cloud of dust billowed across the market

area, covering them and blocking out the sun. Haute coughed, then shouted to the others.

"Move across the market! Use the dust for cover!" This time, his voice seemed muted in the cloud, without an echo. There was a chance that everyone hadn't heard him. His ears were still ringing from the explosion. He assumed others were having the same problem. But they still had to move on.

Haute could barely see Rentahs, who nodded that Haute should lead the way.

The clouds of dust swirled around him, choking him, making him dizzy. That, combined with the throbbing in his head twisted Haute's stomach. He was glad right at that moment that he hadn't eaten much breakfast.

Twice, he tripped and almost fell, once over the arm of a Skaarj. No body attached. Just the arm.

The wind finally drifted the dust and smoke slowly past them as Haute and Rentahs reached the left edge of the main boulevard and took cover in a doorway.

Rentahs watched left, Haute right.

The only sound was an occasional footstep of a Mountain Fighter moving into position. Otherwise, the silence of the castle seemed almost haunted.

As the visibility increased, Haute could see the incredible damage that the blasts had caused. Many walls along the boulevard were nothing more than piles of rubble. Doors had been smashed inward, and where the explosive sticks had hit the street, the stone surface was now a large crater as wide as the entire boulevard and at least ten feet deep.

Haute waited, glancing around, until everyone was again in position. He was starting to doubt the sanity of his plan. The wide boulevard ahead of him looked very, very dangerous. And there were Skaarj up there near the mine, of that there was no doubt.

But there was also a mine full of Nali prisoners, who needed to be freed. And if he retreated now, there was no telling how many of those prisoners would die in that mine during the winter months ahead.

"Two teams up each street!" Haute shouted to the others. "Cover each other. Use explosive sticks only when needed."

Haute glanced at the team across the boulevard from him. Bccui and a young fighter named Regayov.

"Ready," Bccui said, his voice clear in the silence of the castle.

"Move up two doors, and then cover us," Haute said.

Both moved up, running crouched to make smaller targets, checking every door as they passed it. Then they took up positions, and Haute and Rentahs moved forward.

It took them almost five minutes before they were past the large crater, when the first signs of Skaarj resistance appeared. Haute caught a glimpse of a Skaarj fighter hiding in a doorway near the upper end of the boulevard. Where there was one, Haute expected there were more.

Possibly many more.

"Bccui," Haute called, pointing ahead. "Skaarj. Find cover."

Bccui nodded, and both he and Regayov crouched down behind stone doorways.

Haute again pulled out two sticks of explosive. These, plus two more, and he would be out of sticks.

"Can you hit it and get back to cover?" Haute asked

Rentahs as he wound twine around the two sticks. "The blast in this enclosed street will be bad."

"I can," Rentahs said. "Just throw it as far as you can."

Haute laughed. "That I will. Ready?"

Rentahs moved ahead of Haute and leaned against a stone door frame, then brought his rifle up into position. Haute could tell what the young fighter was thinking. He'd fire and then roll back around the frame and down to get out of the direct force of the blast.

"Now!" Haute said. He took one large step forward and with all his might, threw the two sticks as far down the street as he could.

For an instant he wanted to watch, just stand in the street to see how far he had thrown the explosives, to see if they reached the doorway where the Skaarj had disappeared.

Then his brain took over, and he dove for the doorway behind Rentahs, rolling in and up against the wall, his hands over his head, covering his ears.

Rentahs hit his mark again.

The force of the explosion spun the young fighter back into the doorway and down on top of Haute. The impact of the young fighter's body knocked the breath out of Haute. He coughed twice and then got the air moving again.

The air in the closed space around them filled quickly with smoke and dust, so thick Haute wondered how he would ever see again.

Rentahs didn't move, his weight heavy on Haute's legs in the choking darkness.

Haute gently moved the young fighter, checking with his hands to see if he was still alive. For a moment, Haute feared the worst, then he found a heartbeat. Solid and strong.

But Rentahs was bleeding from a wound on the forehead. Obviously, the blast had smashed something into him before he could get behind the door. Or he had hit something on the way in.

Slowly, carefully, he laid Rentahs on the floor in the dark, swirling dust, coughing and choking as he did.

Another explosion rocked the castle, knocking bits of ceiling off onto Haute's head and shoulders, pelting him like a hard rain. Haute couldn't tell from which street that had come. He couldn't even tell where the door to the street was, everything was so black around him.

Then, far in the distance, there was another explosion. It was so far away it barely shook the ground. It took a moment for Haute to understand just what that was. Then he remembered the road. They must have blown up a transport bringing in more Skaarj.

Another distant explosion, and then a close one that again knocked a rain of debris from the ceiling down on them. Haute did his best to cover his own head, and the face and head of Rentahs.

In all his life, Haute had never imagined being in such a fight as this one. He had never imagined being in any fight. Now, it seemed as if the world around him was coming apart in a nightmarish fashion. Death was everywhere. Just like in his visions, blood ran in the rivers and streets.

Haute checked Rentahs as best he could, then looked around through the cloud of dust and smoke, searching for the door to the street. Finally he found it, a faint area of light in the swirling blackness.

Haute picked up Rentahs with his lower arms,

making sure the young fighter's rifle was with him, then headed for the light, moving carefully on the debris that covered the floor.

"Haute!"

Bccui's voice came through the cloud as Haute reached the much lighter street.

"Here," Haute said, lowering Rentahs down next to the wall, unwilling to go too far away from the door and the cover it provided.

A moment later, through the slowly swirling clouds, Bccui and Regayov appeared like ghosts, completely white from the dust. Only their eyes had any color to them. Haute had no doubt he looked the same to them.

"Is he alive?" Bccui asked, bending down beside Haute and checking Rentahs.

"Yes, but I don't know how bad the injury is."

"We need to get him to the meadow," Bccui said.

Haute agreed. Ablee and two of the others waiting there in the support team were experienced in medical. They would know what to do. Haute had no idea.

Around them, the wind was slowly blowing the clouds of dust away, letting the sun break through. Up the boulevard, rifle fire echoed through the streets. But no more explosions.

"I'll take him," Haute said. "I need to get away from the mine, anyway. You go help the others. Free the prisoners in the mine if you can, and then head for the meadow."

Bccui started to object, then stopped.

"Make sure that if there are too many of them," Haute said, "that you retreat."

"We will," Bccui said. He patted Haute on the arm. "See you in the meadow."

With that, Bccui and Regayov turned and started up the boulevard, moving slowly from door to door toward the second explosion crater in the road.

Haute watched them for just a few seconds, then bent down and picked up Rentahs in his lower arms, leaving his upper ones free to hold his rifle. The kid was heavy, almost solid muscle. It was going to be slow going, but he would make it.

He worked his way back down the boulevard, staying as close to the wall as he could.

He stumbled a lot over the debris. Twice, he tripped so bad he almost dropped Rentahs, but each time managed to catch himself and keep moving.

Behind him, the fighting continued, the sounds of rifle fire echoing over the valley. But by the time he had reached the archway, it had slowed.

Outside, moving down the main road away from the castle, he couldn't tell if the fighting had stopped, or if he just couldn't hear it anymore.

At the place where he and Rentahs had dived for the ditch, he left the road and moved up the hill through the field toward the trees.

He never reached them.

He was looking down, making sure where he was stepping in the brush, when suddenly out of the trees Ablee and two of the support team stumbled forward, followed immediately by at least a dozen Skaarj, all with their weapons trained on him.

He stopped, completely shocked, staring at the nightmare in front of him.

It couldn't be happening. He was seeing things.

But then he knew it was real.

Very, very real.

For an instant he thought about firing, taking some of the monsters with him when he died.

Then he realized that if he did, Rentahs in his arms would also die.

He froze, staring at Ablee and the others. Ablee looked as angry as Haute had ever seen him.

If Haute were hit, the two remaining sticks of explosive in his pocket would go off and kill Ablee, as well as Rentahs. And he couldn't do that to his friends.

The vision of his own death flashed through Haute's mind. The three castles at sunrise and then his own death, tied up and burned. There were no more visions left except that one.

And the one of the distant future.

He slowly let the gun drop from his hands into the weeds at his feet. Then, just as slowly, he pushed Rentahs's gun to the ground.

One of the Skaarj motioned for Haute to join Ablee and the others. Then the Skaarj, at least two dozen strong, moved off toward the castle, to recapture what the Mountain Fighters had just worked so hard to take.

Ablee helped Haute lower Rentahs to the ground and quickly checked him. "I think he's going to be all right, for all the good that will do him now."

Haute laughed, a sick laugh that didn't push back the memory of the vision of his own death.

Suddenly, Ablee touched his arm. "Look."

Haute glanced back at the castle. From the upper side of the castle, near the mine, hundreds of Nali prisoners were streaming out of a side entrance and toward the trees, away from the mine and the castle.

While the prisoners ran, six or seven Mountain Fighters were firing in defense at the advancing Skaarj, giving the prisoners time to get into the trees and get started toward the summit.

Haute, even from this distance, could see Bccui and Targee, fighting on, saving hundreds.

Haute had never felt such pride before. Pride in what he had done. Pride in his people.

For what seemed like forever, but actually lasted only a fraction of a minute, the fight continued, the advancing Skaarj firing on the retreating Mountain Fighters.

Finally, the last of the prisoners and fighters disappeared into the trees, and the fighting stopped.

Ablee glanced at Haute. "Well, friend, it's no longer up to us, is it?"

Haute stared at the place in the forest where the last of the prisoners had disappeared into the trees, followed quickly by his brother and the other Mountain Fighters.

"Watch," Haute said to Ablee. He had a hunch what was going to happen next.

Suddenly from out of the trees one last beam of rifle fire shot toward the advancing Skaarj. Then a huge explosion rocked the field and the side of the castle. The ground under Haute shook. That must have been at least three sticks of explosive power wrapped together.

A huge cloud of dust filled the air, then slowly drifted toward the trees.

Ablee laughed and patted Haute on the back. The explosion had killed at least half of the advancing Skaarj. The other half were now holding their positions, no longer following the prisoners and the Mountain Fighters.

Haute looked up at the ugly orange and yellow and green skin of the Skaarj guard standing over them. There was a red aura around the monster. A blood aura that Haute wanted to wipe off the face of the planet.

"We won this battle today," Haute said to Ablee. "There will be many fighters in those rescued prisoners."

"More than enough to replace us," Ablee said.

"More than enough," Haute said. "But our fighting days are over."

In his head a very clear voice said simply,

Yes.

And no.

Chapter 16

Second Occupation

Karrikta paced back and forth in the command center, waiting for the raiding party to report. It had been half an hour since they had entered the cave; what was keeping them?

He'd been lucky the razorfly had spotted the Hhumans as it followed the path of the stolen flyer. Also lucky it could plant a homing beacon on the back of the resistance leader's vehicle when they made their rendezvous. The beacon had stopped transmitting the moment it had been submerged, but it had led the scouts close enough to spot a cave entrance high up on a mountainside above the lake. Karrikta couldn't count on further good fortune; he had ordered all of the scouts to attack at once, to surprise the Nali and wipe out their headquarters before they knew they had been discovered.

The scouts had flown straight into the cave, and that's the last Karrikta had heard from them. The rock mass blocked direct transmission, so they couldn't report their progress, but they should have been able to fight their way all the way through the mountain by now. Something had gone wrong.

"Send in another team," he ordered his battle commander. "I want to know what's going on in there."

"Yes, sir."

The commander examined his situation monitor to see who was closest, but before he could relay the order, the surveillance tech who had been watching by satellite said, "I see motion. They're coming out. Six, eight, ten—wait. There weren't that many flyers."

"What?" Karrikta stomped over behind him and looked into the monitor himself.

A steady stream of vehicles shot out of the cave mouth, angling away in all directions once they had cleared it. These weren't just passenger vehicles, either; most of them bore turret guns or held bombs slung beneath their fuselages.

"Reduce magnification," he said. The tech complied, and the stream of vehicles became a tiny thread of silver dots, but now they could see dozens more streams just like it issuing from all over the mountain. It looked like a volcano about to blow, venting steam from every crack just before it erupted.

"Check the lake," he said, and when the tech moved the view over, they saw that the lake surface was aboil with escaping vehicles.

"Track them!" Karrikta ordered, but the tech said, "There're too many, sir. They're splitting up."

"Then get warplanes in there," he ordered the battle commander. "Shoot down anything that flies."

"Yes, sir," the commander said, but they both knew it was a futile gesture. Hundreds of vehicles had already escaped, and hundreds more would go before the planes could get there. Even then, what could eight do against so many? That was the extent of the true Skaarj military power on Na Pali—eight suborbital warplanes. With the Nali so effectively crushed years ago, there had been no need for more, and the homeworld had other wars to fight, elsewhere.

He wouldn't get all eight of them, either. Rrajigar wasn't the only city on Na Pali, and Karrikta wasn't the only security chief with a problem. "Send word to the other commanders," he said. "Tell them what's happening."

He smacked a fist against his chest. He knew how this would look to the others. He had lost his chance to crush the resistance with a single blow. He had underestimated his enemy, and he had paid the price.

He would pay more in the days to come, too. Of that he was certain. With their cover blown, the Nali had no choice but to strike soon, before the Skaarj could hunt them down one at a time. Rrajigar was the closest city, so that's where they would almost certainly direct their attack.

That's how Karrikta would do it, anyway. He wondered if the Nali thought the same way. And what of the Hhumans? They were still a complete mystery. Would they rush straight from one battle into another?

"Get our defenses ready," he said. "I want antiaircraft weapons on every rooftop, and I want troops guarding every path up the side of the mesa. Put advance scouts in the foothills, and order everyone to shoot any alien on sight."

"Yes, sir," said the commander, and other voices echoed his.

The command center hummed with activity as

everyone rushed to implement his orders. There was an air of excitement in the room. Indeed, when Karrikta looked out the wraparound windows at the city below him, he sensed that same feeling throughout the city. Security forces struggled to haul bulky weapons up onto roofs; others who had already set up their stations fired test shots into the air; he saw soldiers laughing and slapping one another on the back. He knew what they were saying: "At last we get to fight a real battle!"

Idiots. This resembled a real battle about as much as they resembled real soldiers. That was the only thing that would save their worthless hides in the hours to come. They had no more enemy here than they had experience fighting one. Since the occupation, years before anyone here was born, Na Pali had been a training ground for new recruits and a convenient place to stash people who didn't fit in, back home. It was a big-game preserve for those who wanted to hunt intelligent prey. It hadn't taken anything more to hold the planet against the Nali, so nothing more had been provided.

It wasn't as bad now as it had been before Karrikta arrived. In his seven years here, he had whipped this collection of misfits into as decent a fighting force as possible, given the circumstances, but they lacked one crucial ingredient: experience.

They were about to gain that. Unfortunately, the least experienced of the lot were the ones with him there in the command center. He had decided not to waste battle talent in management, but now, as he looked at the technicians and accountants around him—half of them not even armed—he wondered at the wisdom of that.

Too late to restructure now. One of the surveillance techs said, "Incoming air traffic, southwest quarter, vector four."

Karrikta looked out the window to the southwest, ticked off four-sixths of the distance from south to west—squinting into the sun, which was just sliding behind the peaks—and there he spotted a tiny glint of silver bobbing and weaving its way down out of the mountains. The pilot had to have flown directly here from the cave at top speed to make it this quickly. So they were going for a direct assault.

"Battle stations," he ordered. "Get ready for more."

Then, because he knew that attitude won half of any fight, he said, "At last, we get to fight a real battle!"

Everyone cheered. They cheered again when a plasma bolt lanced out toward the approaching flyer, even though it fizzled way short of the target. The flyer came steadily on, growing from a featureless dot to a sleek teardrop shape with two tarydium cannons mounted on the ends of stubby wings. It opened fire just as prematurely, its shots arching downward to stitch a twin line of explosions through the badlands below the mesa on which Rrajigar stood.

Someone out there in the line of fire shot straight upward with a hand weapon; the energy pulse looked like a tiny scratch of light that winked out when the flyer's shots reached it.

First casualty, thought Karrikta. Not counting the scouts who had undoubtedly perished in the cave.

The flyer came on without dodging, even when more and more weapons opened fire on it. As it drew closer, the sky lit up with so many energy beams and timed tarydium explosions that they hid their target. Karrikta could feel the vibration from the firing of the guns on the roof above the command center, and he could see streaks flying past from rooftops below and to the side.

"Good grief," he said. "Tell those idiots to save some ammunition for the next one."

He heard orders being issued, and suddenly the firing stopped. Except for the attacking flyer; it blew through the wall of smoke with its cannons still blazing, and now it was within range. The twin lines of explosions splashed across the river and climbed the slope toward the city.

"Well, *somebody* shoot it!" Karrikta said.

More frantic orders, then the barrage opened up again. The flyer was completely vaporized in an instant, but not before its cannon shots took out a building on the edge of town. Karrikta squinted to see. Flaming debris rained down on neighboring rooftops—some of them occupied.

First blood for both sides.

"More approaching," the surveillance tech said. "Seven targets, all southwest quadrant."

"Get ready for them," Karrikta said. "Commanders, call your shots this time."

They couldn't see the approaching aircraft through the smoke of the first one's destruction. There was a light evening breeze blowing down out of the mountains; that would eventually clear away the smoke, but not soon enough. Fortunately, some of the guns had radar, and some of the missiles they fired had tarydium-seeking warheads, but the planet's natural tarydium levels meant the warheads' sensitivity had to be set so low that they were nearly useless.

There wasn't an infinite supply of warheads, either.

Karrikta watched the satellite view as the seven enemy flyers approached the city. They didn't fly in formation. From the way they weaved back and forth, it didn't look as though their pilots were capable of it. Unless they thought they were taking evasive action, in which case they were equally pitiful, just in a different way. They'd have to do a lot better than that to evade a guided missile.

They came within range of the longest-reaching guns. A few shots climbed into the sky, much more measured this time, and three of the seven flyers exploded before they even knew they were targeted.

The others opened fire. Four, eight, twelve missiles lanced out toward the city. Karrikta looked out the windows to see if he could spot them, but the smoke still obscured the view.

The radar-guided guns could see through it well enough. Nine of the missiles and two more flyers added bright flashes and more smoke to the thickening cloud.

The other two incoming missiles flashed past the defenders and smashed into the power plant, one striking the cooling tower and the other making a direct hit on the generator station. The lights in the command center went out, and all the monitoring equipment died, but a moment later it all came back on as the backup power supply in the basement switched on.

Lights blinked all over the city, but every building had its own generator. Nobody had trusted the Nali technology enough to rely on it completely. That, at least, had been a smart decision.

The computers needed time to reset; in the meantime, Karrikta was reduced to watching out the window as bright lights lanced up and down through the evening sky. The last two flyers were finally hit, one of them spiraling in to splash into the river, but the other one had enough momentum to carry it into the city. It crashed into one of the five towers, punching through the wall before it exploded. Rather than tip over, the tower simply collapsed straight down. Karrikta watched two of the soldiers on the roof leap to their deaths, but the ones who stayed fared no better. The tower disappeared into a billowing cloud of flame and smoke, and its final impact shook the command center hard enough to rattle fangs.

The fire lit up the ceiling with flickering orange light. It looked like the entire sky was reflecting it, but that was just the sunset. There was less than an hour of daylight left.

Karrikta wondered if the Nali would continue to attack through the night. He wasn't sure they would need to, if things continued the way they were going.

The computers came back on line. "More coming," said the surveillance tech. "Nine this time, four in one cluster, five in another."

"Where are those damned warplanes?" Karrikta demanded.

"One's coming in from the east right now," said the battle commander.

"Good." Karrikta watched it in the satellite monitor as it swept around Rrajigar to the north, making a wide arc westward so it could attack the incoming flyers from out of the sun. It flashed toward them at twice their speed, firing its plasma cannon at them in swift, precise jabs. Each shot took out a flyer; the group of five disappeared in rapid succession. The other four split up, but their destruction took only a little longer. Their debris rained down in the foothills, setting fires far from Rrajigar.

The warplane circled slowly around the city, darting out to shoot down anything else that approached. Karrikta relaxed a little as he watched it dispatch another attacker with a single shot. Maybe things weren't as hopeless as he had thought.

Chapter 17

First Occupation

Three days after the Mountain Fighters had captured and controlled the three castles south of Rennod Pass, Haute sat in the shade of a tree on that pass, staring north toward the main Skaarj compounds. To his right, the remains of two Skaarj transports were like skeletons of dead animals bleaching in the sun. The Skaarj bodies had been dragged off into the trees and tossed in a mass grave, their weapons and other useful items on the transports salvaged and carried off the pass.

Around him, the day was blazing hot and very dry. He had almost gone through his allotted amount of water for the day. With this heat, and at this altitude, he was going to need more. All the fighters up here guarding the pass were going to need more water. He would talk to Jeeie and make sure that happened.

The fight to take the southern castles had gone just as Haute and the others had planned. Targee had intercepted the transport and destroyed it. Bccui and his fighters had captured their objective, then moved down the road and set a trap for the Skaarj reinforcements coming from the south. They had taken them without a scratch, simply blowing the transport off the road with two sticks of explosives. Then they had easily recaptured the southernmost castle, killing off the last Skaarj south of the pass.

The defenders of the pass had also done their job, destroying both transports coming from the north. They had killed twelve Skaarj without any problem, simply by planting explosive sticks in the dirt of the road and firing at the sticks as the transports passed over the top. It was a method the Skaarj were just completely unprepared for. It seemed, so far, that the Skaarj just didn't expect the Nali to fight at all. But no doubt they had now learned that was no longer the case.

Haute couldn't believe that they had actually won this first battle. There wasn't a Skaarj anywhere south of the Rennod Pass, and he planned on keeping it that way.

In the distance, Haute could see a large meadow, the gleaming white of the tailings pile of a tarydium mine, and the shape of a castle. From Jeeie's scouts, he knew the Skaarj were mounting a counterattack, getting ready there. Haute had no idea why they would even try. So far, in trying to control the three castles to the south of the pass, the Skaarj had lost more than fifty fighters out of the two hundred or so that had been in the crashed ship. And not one Mountain Fighter had even received more than a cut. There just weren't that many Skaarj on the planet to hold everything. And it made no sense for them to try.

But they were going to, more than likely sometime

in the next three days. So Haute had decided that they wouldn't get the chance to even mount an attack. He would hit them in their preparation area.

The castles and the area south of this pass had to stay protected and in Nali control. There was no other way to survive the coming winter. Jeeie had made that clear to him in a private conversation. The food and supplies in the area around the caverns just wasn't enough to support a population nearing three hundred.

Haute knew that while he sat here on the pass, many members of the caverns' population were moving into the castle Wocsom. Only about fifty would remain in the caverns as support to the fighters. Elutie, his brother's wife, his ex-girlfriend, was moving with the children to the castle. And Haute hoped that his parents, if they were still hiding in the hills to the south, would return to the castle and join Bccui and Elutie.

He knew he never would.

So, to protect his own family and the other Nali who couldn't fight, the pass and the castles south of the pass, had to be defended. Attacking first, before the Skaarj could figure how to get past the Nali defenses, was the best way, in Haute's opinion.

As with some of Haute's other decisions, this one Ablee had shouted his opposition to. Haute had again talked him down, calming his old friend, making him see that the only way to do it was as Haute had planned. And since so many of the residents of the caverns were leaving for the castle, Ablee had decided to come along on this mission, as support. He wouldn't fight, but he would cook, carry supplies, and help with the wounded if needed.

"We're ready," Rentahs said behind Haute.

"Are you sure about this, Haute?" Ablee asked as he came up beside Rentahs.

Haute pushed himself to his feet and smiled at his friend. "As sure as I've ever been."

Ablee nodded. "Then let's go."

Without even so much as a glance back at the pass, Haute, with Ablee at his side, led Targee, Bccui, Rentahs, and twenty Mountain Fighters down the mountain toward the distant castle. Again, he knew he would never return.

He didn't know how he knew, exactly. But he knew.

He also knew from his visions that he had one more castle to see at sunrise. And he knew that castle waited in the valley in the distance.

The sunrise would be tomorrow morning.

He was right.

The vision came true.

At sunrise the following morning, Haute was hiding under a large pine, staring out over a shallow valley. Stretched out before him was a very active castle, with Skaarj guards walking along the outside castle walls, and Nali coming and going from the mine.

Haute had no hope that any of the Nali prisoners would help in the coming fight. He just hoped that he could save many of their lives, and maybe help some of them escape over the pass.

He studied the situation for a few minutes, then silently retreated back into the trees, moving back to a place near a mound of rocks that was the agreed-upon meeting place.

As he arrived, Rentahs and Targee appeared out of the trees to his right.

"Roads are ready," Targee said.

Haute nodded. Rentahs and Targee had planted numbers of explosive sticks at four places along the road leading into the castle from the other Skaarj strongholds to the north. Two Mountain Fighters hidden in locations near those sticks had orders to blow up any transport that tried to pass, then to vanish into the trees and return to the pass.

"How many Skaarj are in there?" Haute asked, glancing at Jeeie.

"Best estimates are at least forty," Jeeie said. "Most seem to be stationed back near the mine area. But by now, they'll be moving around everywhere."

Haute nodded. "Any idea where the Nali are kept?"

"Working in the mine from dawn to dusk," Jeeie said. "Almost no exceptions."

Haute nodded. "Good, they will be out of the way."

He glanced around at the fighters gathered there. For two days, they had all practiced throwing explosive sticks and hitting them with a blast from the Skaarj rifle. The same method Haute and Rentahs had used in the last fight.

This time they would all use it, from different positions around the castle. Then they'd fall back to the pass.

Hit and run. That was the plan.

Haute smiled at all the fighters around him. "Everyone has fifteen minutes to get into position. Wait for the first blast."

There didn't seem to be any questions from anyone, so Haute said, "Good luck. We'll meet back on the pass."

Silently, in teams of two, the fighters turned and moved off into the trees, spreading around the castle under the cover of the forest. The attack on the castle was going to come from all directions at once. Haute had had no dream that they would capture the castle. But they most certainly would make a dent in the Skaarj forces here.

Haute glanced at Ablee, who remained with the six others who were functioning as a support group. "Better take your crew back to the meadow."

The meadow was a small opening in the trees about half the distance back toward the pass. Ablee had agreed to wait there and to help anyone up the mountain that needed help.

Ablee nodded. "Good luck."

Haute smiled. "See you shortly."

Ablee turned and headed off through the trees, the other crew members following him. After a few moments, only Haute and Rentahs remained.

"Guess it's time," Haute said.

Rentahs smiled. "Shall we go kill some Skaarj?"

Haute laughed. "With pleasure."

Ten minutes later, they had worked their way up to a position overlooking the front archway of the castle. The Skaarj had brought two transports out of the front archway and were working on them in some fashion. Skaarj patrolled the walls, and other Skaarj were posted in the towers, rifles aimed out over the open areas. It was those guards that Haute worried about the most. From that high, they had clear shots at everything around the castle.

Haute pointed at the transports and Rentahs nodded. If Haute stood and threw the stick hard, he just might be able to get one there. Then the question was, could Rentahs hit it from that distance? Was he that good a shot?

They were about to find out.

Haute pulled three explosive sticks from his pack and held two in a left hand while he grasped the third in his upper right hand, ready to throw. When standing, he would throw three, one right after the other. If he was fast enough, all three would be in the air before the first was exploded by Rentahs.

They were going to have to move quickly. The guards from the tower would be blanketing this area, focusing their attention here before the others around the castle attacked.

Rentahs stood, his back to a large tree, rifle in his hand.

Haute glanced at him. "Ready?" he whispered.

Rentahs checked the charge on the rifle, then nodded.

Before he had time to think about what exactly he was doing, and just how stupid it might be, Haute jumped to his feet, stepped forward, and with all his might tossed the first stick at the transport.

Beside him, Rentahs stepped out from the tree and followed the stick through the air with the barrel of the rifle.

Haute threw a second stick.

Out of the corner of his eye, Haute could see that two of the guards in the towers had spotted them and were turning toward them.

Haute threw the third stick, then swung his rifle around off his shoulder and brought it up just as Rentahs fired his first shot.

The shot hit the first stick just as it landed near the transports.

Perfect throw, perfect shot.

The explosion flipped over the two transports like child's toys, rolling them back toward the main archway of the castle. The Skaarj working on the transports were blown apart, parts of their bodies tumbling in all directions.

The blast smashed into them, causing Haute to stagger backward for a second.

He regained his footing and fired at the explosion at the same time Rentahs did, holding down the trigger and sweeping the energy beam from his rifle along the ground in the area where the other explosive sticks should have landed.

One of their shots found its target, causing another, second, huge explosion.

Suddenly, the tree limbs over his head cracked and snapped, showering him with pine needles.

One of the guards on the tower had fired, missing high.

Both Haute and Rentahs ducked behind the trunks of large trees as more shots smashed into the area around them, kicking up dirt and burning through brush as if it didn't exist. Luckily, both the trees they were behind were large enough to withstand a Skaarj rifle blast.

Haute found himself breathing hard, his heart pounding in his chest so hard it seemed to want to jump right out. That was the first time, in all the fights, that a Skaarj had actually fired directly at him. The first time that he might have been killed.

His stomach twisted as the vision of his coming death overwhelmed him. The intense pain, the fire, the burning.

It flooded over him, freezing him in position.

Another shot cut at the tree he hid behind, sending smoke pouring into the air, swirling around him in a choking cloud.

Then suddenly the ground under them shook as explosion after explosion rocked the castle.

The attack was on.

Haute forced himself to take a deep breath and to shove the images of his own death to the back of his mind. Right now, there were important things to do. And he couldn't be thinking about his own death while doing them.

He focused his thoughts back on the fight. From the sounds of the explosions, the practice of throwing and then hitting the explosive sticks had worked.

Haute waited a long count of three as the smoke swirled around him from the burning tree over his head, then he ducked sideways and down behind a small rock where he could see.

What he saw made him want to shout for joy.

The castle was almost completely covered in a massive cloud of dust and smoke. One of the taller castle towers, where a Skaarj had been posted, was no longer in existence, knocked completely down by an explosion.

From the back of the castle, another explosion rocked the ground, sending more of the dust and smoke swirling. It seemed that some of the fighters were not following orders exactly. They were staying and continuing to pound the Skaarj with more explosions and rifle fire.

Haute understood exactly how they felt. If he could see a Skaarj moving right now, he would also be attacking.

As Haute watched, the wind blew the cloud of dust to the left, exposing part of the castle and then slowly the main archway. Dead or wounded Skaarj lay around the archway. Haute could see nothing moving inside.

Targee and another fighter appeared behind them, looking winded and excited.

Haute climbed to his feet and stepped back to meet the two, leaving Rentahs with his rifle pointed at the castle.

"You up for a little more?" Haute asked Targee.

He smiled. "We could take this place."

"My thoughts exactly," Haute said, glancing back at the castle. The attack had turned out to be much, much more effective than he had hoped. And there were a large number of Nali in the mine that needed to be released. Maybe even some of them would turn into fighters.

"Find anyone else who wants to help," Haute said to Targee. "I'm going down a little closer."

With a glance at Rentahs, who only smiled and nodded his agreement, Haute spun out from behind the trees and headed out into the open toward the main archway, running bent over to make a smaller target.

Rentahs' almost silent footsteps were right behind him.

He half expected some fire from the towers, or that suddenly a dozen Skaarj would appear in front of him, guns ready to cut him into pieces.

Nothing.

One of the wounded Skaarj just inside the archway moved a little, but didn't stand.

Haute found a small ditch alongside the road, about twenty paces directly in front of the main archway. He rolled down into it and Rentahs joined him, keeping his rifle trained on the castle.

Haute quickly pulled two more explosive sticks from his pack. He wrapped a small piece of twine around them to hold them together, then patted Rentahs. "This will be a big one."

"Go," Rentahs said.

Haute raised up on his knees and threw the two sticks through the archway and onto the stone of the market area.

As the two sticks hit the ground, Rentahs fired, sweeping the sticks with a solid beam of destruction.

The explosion flattened Haute down into the ditch and knocked Rentahs over backward. The wounded Skaarj who had been off at one side of the archway was tossed into the air and smashed into the remains of one of the transports.

Large stones from the archway tumbled to the ground, smashing into pieces.

As the huge cloud of smoke and dust drifted over the castle, Haute eased up and looked around behind them. Targee and five others were running across the open meadow toward him from the right. And Bccui and another fighter were coming toward him from the left.

Ten fighters to storm the castle.

Out of the trees, four others appeared, running low along the side of the stone castle wall. It seemed that the word had passed through all the fighters.

"We've got help," Haute said to Rentahs as he scrambled to his feet and ran until he reached the stone wall, stopping there with his back against the hard surface, waiting until the others had taken up positions.

Bccui moved up and took a position beside Haute. "You sure we should be doing this? There's still a lot of Skaarj alive in there."

"So we have to go in there to kill them," Haute said.

Bccui smiled. "That we do. I don't suppose you might have a plan?"

Haute glanced around at the men in covered positions around him. "Stay two by two," he said, loud enough for all of them to hear. "We'll work our way up the three main roads by exploding sticks ahead of us and waiting until the dust clears before advancing."

"Good," Targee said and the others nodded that they understood.

"Watch the doors and behind you," Bccui said.

"At the slightest sign of trouble," Haute said, "we run for the forest and meet on the pass. Understand?"

Again, everyone did. But Haute knew that they would follow him, forward or backward. For him, there was no backward. Only forward.

To his own death.

Chapter 18

Second Occupation

Melnori tried not to despair at the sight of all the weapons. The walls were festooned with handguns, rifles, and less obvious devices, and cabinets held enough ammunition for them to stock the entire resistance. He knew he should be thankful that such a hoard had landed in his lap at such an opportune time, but he couldn't work up the enthusiasm to rejoice at the prospect of so much destructive power.

He couldn't ignore the truth: all of this had been brought to Na Pali by aliens who were just as eager as the Skaarj to exploit the planet for its tarydium.

He wished, not for the first time, that he could find some way to convert tarydium into worthless rock. Without its lure, Na Pali would be of no interest to anyone but the Nali, who would love the planet even more for its lack of the troublesome element. The sensitive ones, who felt such intense pain in its presence, could finally live in comfort, and the rest of the population could live in peace.

Even the rain of starships would stop, although if Na Pali regained even a fraction of the grandeur it had possessed millennia ago, there would be starships aplenty—all filled with tourists.

That thought nearly made Melnori laugh. The idea that Na Pali would ever mean anything but tarydium to anybody was a lunatic dream. The only tourists the planet was likely to see in his lifetime were Skaarj slavemasters, come to pick over the remnants of Nali civilization after it died in tonight's improbable battle.

Gerick and Quoin were picking through the weapons with the finicky attitude of someone who doesn't want to carry anything he doesn't have to. From their heated discussion in the far corner of the armory, it looked like they had come to a difficult choice, but they turned away from whatever they were arguing about when Zofia returned.

Something seemed different about her. Melnori couldn't say just what it was, but she carried herself differently than she had before. He had seen a similar change when Boris had died. Something had just affected her profoundly, but when she spoke, she said nothing of it.

"The Skaarj messed up the controls pretty badly," she said. "We might be able to fix 'em, but not tonight. Radio's out, too. What have you found?"

"Camouflage armor," Gerick said, turning around—and disappearing. "Plus a ton of weapons, but nothing really new. The Skaarj weapons are better than these." His voice shifted sideways as he spoke, and he flickered into visibility again a few steps away from where he had been.

"Too bad," she said. "The armor's good, though. Where's mine?"

"There're bins of 'em over there," Gerick said, pointing. "Pick one. It's stretchy; one size fits all." He pulled the transparent fabric away from his chest, let it snap back into place.

"Doesn't look much like armor," Zofia observed.

"We fired a few rounds at an empty one, and it held up," Gerick told her. "It stiffens like steel for a second when it's hit. Laser didn't penetrate, either. Quoin's plasma gun toasted the electronics, but it didn't go through."

"Impressive." Zofia dug into the bins and pulled out a bodysuit. It looked to Melnori like a discarded human skin, complete with head. Zofia stuck her feet down through its open face and slid them through the body into the legs, then wiggled her arms into their proper places and pulled the headpiece up over her hair.

"Where's the on/off switch?" she asked.

"Belly button."

She looked down, saw the black dot there, and pushed. She disappeared except for the oval of her face.

"You've got to pull the hood down," Gerick told her.

"Oh." She reached up and tugged a line of invisibility over her eyes, nose, mouth, and finally her chin. Melnori could see a faint shimmer of motion at her neck as she tucked the flap in. "How do I get to my— oh, I see. Slits in the sides." One of her human-made guns appeared at her side, then disappeared again.

"Quoin, Melnori, have you guys got one?" she asked.

Quoin bent a wing and pushed a spot beneath his neck. He vanished, then returned again a moment later. Melnori pushed the button on his chest. Nothing changed from his perspective, but suddenly Zofia laughed.

"I see your extra pair of arms," she said.

"They aren't 'extra,' I assure you," Melnori said. He fumbled with his suit, which he had only partially donned, and pushed the black button on the flap that he had left untucked.

"Ah, that's got it. Great. Looks like we won't have to climb up the mesa inside a water pipe, after all."

Quoin whistled softly. "Do you know that these suits are invisible to the Skaarj? They see a different spectrum than you do."

"Damn, you're right. We won't know until we try it. And I suppose it's stupid to try it until we absolutely have to."

"Perhaps not," said Quoin. "Stupid only if the Skaarj in question could hurt you if it turns out he can see you."

Gerick looked at him. "You know one who couldn't?"

Another low whistle. "We can make one wherever there is a lone soldier."

"How?"

"Come, I will show you. Provided we're finished here."

"Yeah, I've got all I can carry. Zofia, you probably want to grab a laser, at least. They're on that rack right beside you."

"Okay." A sleek hand weapon wiggled, then disappeared as she grasped it. The guns had been treated with a camouflage coating, too.

Quoin stepped toward the door. Gerick followed him, then stopped and turned around. "Are you com—oof!"

Zofia giggled, then she shimmered into existence

right behind him. "Melnori?" she asked. She turned toward him and extended her arm, feeling the air. He resisted the urge to walk around her and tap her on the shoulder from behind; instead, he pressed the two control spots again and switched off the camouflage.

Quoin led them back to his landing craft. It was getting dark enough that his ship was just a silhouette against the deep purple sky. The ground was pitch-black already, and stars were coming out overhead. They climbed aboard, and when they were all crouched down in their places, he took off toward Rrajigar. They could see the battle from quite a distance as flashes of energy lit up the sky. Melnori thought it actually looked rather pretty from this distance. If by some miracle they won, they would have to stage something like it for the rest of the Nali to see, maybe hold some kind of celebration at night and blow up something in memory of the battle of Rrajigar.

Quoin peered at his monitors and slowed his ship well short of the city. "There's one," he said.

He angled the lander down in a steep dive. "What are you going to do?" asked Gerick.

"Capture a Skaarj."

"Just like that?"

"I have practiced this maneuver many times. It never fails."

"Knock wood," Zofia said, rapping her head with her curled fingers. Melnori had no idea what that meant, but now was not the time to ask. Quoin swept the ship down toward the dark ground, watching the monitors rather than the night outside the actual windshield. Melnori could see a reverse silhouette of a Skaarj—a bright, blurry outline of one—standing at attention with his arms at his sides, peering out into the darkness. At the last moment, the figure became aware of the vehicle swooping down on him; Melnori saw him whirl and raise his arm to fire, but he was too late. The image swelled to fill the screen, and a soft *thump* shook the ship at the same moment.

Quoin angled around in a steep turn, then swept toward the same spot again. The monitor showed the Skaarj sprawled on the ground, not moving.

"Good grief," Zofia said. "You just drop down and whack 'em on the head?"

"That is how my people hunt," Quoin said. He brought the lander down beside the Skaarj, trained a spotlight on him, and climbed out of the seat. "Let us see if our camouflage suits work."

All four of them activated their armor, then bumped and jostled their way into the airlock. They stepped out cautiously, but it soon became apparent that the Skaarj was out cold. In fact, he looked dead.

"I think you killed him," Melnori said.

"Impossible. I have done this many times." Quoin walked up to the Skaarj and kicked a foot. It twitched, but the Skaarj didn't wake up.

"What I haven't done before is bind one. We need rope." His voice drifted away, then a coil of silvery cord floated out of the airlock. "Safety tether should do," he said. The rope moved over toward the Skaarj, and Quoin said, "Help hold his arms together behind his back."

Melnori moved closer, bumped into Zofia or Gerick—he couldn't tell which—and grasped the Skaarj's left arm. It was the closest he had ever come to a live one, and as close as he ever wanted to. The skin was hot to the touch, a product of tarydium-based high metabolism, yet it still felt wet and slimy.

One of the invisible humans held the other arm,

and Quoin wrapped the cord around the wrists, tying both arms tight behind the Skaarj's back. They tied the feet together, as well, then bound hands and feet together and left the Skaarj on his side.

"One moment." Quoin went into the airlock again, then returned with a plastic bottle. The top was unscrewed and the bottle tilted over the Skaarj's head, splashing water in his face.

The Skaarj woke with a roar, then roared again when he realized he was tied up. Melnori stepped backward and reached for his stunner, but stopped before withdrawing it.

"Who's there?" the Skaarj demanded.

At Melnori's right, Gerick scuffed his feet, and the Skaarj tilted his head back to look toward the sound. "Show yourself!" he demanded.

"Let's try full spectrum light," Quoin said, then he spoke a few hissing, clicking syllables in his native language. The light grew yellower, warmer.

The Skaarj tugged at his bonds, kicked himself around in a circle. "Who are you?" he roared.

"Your worst nightmare," Gerick said. Suddenly a beam of laser light shot out from a spot only an arm's length away from the Skaarj's face, just missing his knees as it traveled the length of his body.

Instead of flinching, the Skaarj jackknifed forward and snapped his powerful jaws at the source of the light.

"Yow!" Gerick yelled. Melnori heard him fall down, then scramble back into the darkness.

"Are you hurt?" he asked, just as Zofia said, "Gerick!"

"I'm all right. Startled me is all."

"Who are you?" the Skaarj demanded again. "Show yourselves, cowards!"

"I think we've proved they work," Quoin said. "Anybody hungry?"

"What?" Melnori asked. "You can't seriously . . ." He couldn't bring himself to say it.

"What else do you think I do with them? My kind need fresh meat, and lots of it." A plasma pistol slid into view as Quoin drew it from beneath his camouflage.

"Don't—" Melnori said, but it was too late. There was a bright flash, and when his eyes recovered, the Skaarj had no head.

Quoin flickered into view again and holstered his pistol. Then, walking up to the Skaarj's body, he pulled his wings free of the camouflage suit and used his claws to rip open the Skaarj's powerful chest.

"Here," he said, holding a strip of steaming flesh out toward Melnori. "It'll put some spring in your step."

"No, thank you," Melnori said, fighting down the urge to gag.

Quoin said, "Where I come from, we share the flesh of our enemies before a battle. It's mostly symbolic, but there's a strong basis in practicality for it. We use their energy against them."

He held the meat out toward where the humans had last been. Not surprisingly, Gerick switched off his camouflage and took it from him.

"You mind if I cook it?" he asked.

"Not at all." Quoin ripped free another section and held it out. "Zofia?"

"Uhh . . . I guess. It's not like he's human or anything." She blinked into being again and took the meat gingerly between two fingers.

Quoin ripped free another strip for himself.

Gerick still had his laser out. He twisted a silver

ring at the end of it and fired the beam again, and this time the light fanned out in a cone. He dangled the meat a hand's width in front of the muzzle for a few seconds, and it sizzled and popped as it cooked.

Zofia did the same; then the two of them raised their cooked strips of Skaarj toward each other, and Zofia said in a voice that sounded a bit nervous, "Here's to victory."

They each took a cautious bite. Quoin gobbled his in one gulp and ripped free another strip.

"Hmm," said Zofia. "Not bad. Tastes a little like chicken."

"What is chicken?" Quoin asked.

"It's a—" She stopped. "It's a kind of rodent we have on Earth. Right, Gerick?"

"Right," he said quickly.

Melnori could tell they were lying, but he couldn't think of a good reason why. What did it matter what chicken was?

"Well, eat your fill," Quoin said. "There's plenty here for everybody. And then I imagine it's about time to get you three to Rrajigar."

"You *three?*" asked Melnori. "Aren't you going in with us?"

"Are you kidding? And waste all the work I've done on my ship? As soon as I drop you off, I'm going to take it out and knock down some aircraft. Give the rest of your fleet a better chance to get through."

"Oh," said Melnori. Yes, that sounded like a good idea. He wouldn't have thought of that on his own. He didn't think like these others; that was clear.

As he watched them eat the Skaarj, he counted himself lucky.

Chapter 19

First Occupation

The Skaarj loaded Haute, Ablee, Rentahs, and the other three captured Mountain Fighters on the back of a transport and started off toward the north. Haute did his best to brace himself and the still unconscious Rentahs against the side metal wall of the transport, to reduce the number of bumps and the amount of jar, but he had very little luck. The road just wasn't meant for such vehicles. Every hole, every root, every rock seemed to jar right to Haute's core. After an hour, he felt completely bruised and sore.

The Skaarj guarding them smelled of tarydium dust and a sickly sour smell that Haute remembered from his vision. The combination of the closeness of the Skaarj and the transport was slowly increasing his pounding headache. Something about the Skaarj and tarydium: the mineral was either a major part of their blood, or the strange pack-looking things on their backs were something run by tarydium. For all Haute knew, the Skaarj themselves ran on tarydium, considering how they were forcing the Nali to work the mines.

Either way, Haute was allergic to any Skaarj.

So was Ablee. As the hours passed, Ablee was having more and more trouble breathing. There would be no telling what would happen to him when they reached a castle.

Haute did his best not to let the vision of his own death control his thoughts. He had no doubt that he was about to die. But he didn't *have* to focus on it. Instead, he forced himself to think about the victories.

First, they had driven the Skaarj from the three southern castles. It would be very, very difficult for the Skaarj to ever retake them. Second, today they had, more than likely, stopped the Skaarj from attacking over the pass any time in the future. Third, of the two hundred or so Skaarj that had originally been in the crashed spaceship, more than sixty of them were now dead.

But that left more than one hundred and forty.

Haute instantly pushed that thought from his head. There undoubtedly would be more fighters among the prisoners released today. Fighters who would, after having been slaves, very much want to continue the job he and Ablee had started. Haute also knew that someday, in the not too distant future, the new fighters would finish it. They would drive the Skaarj from the planet. And it would be centuries before they returned.

Two hours after they had started, the transport sputtered, lurched twice, and stopped.

The sudden stillness seemed almost shocking to Haute. The silence of the forest around them seemed to overwhelm them, like a flood held back for too long. The pounding in Haute's head eased just a little. He wasn't sure if that was from the lack of noise and the jerking motion, or from the transport motor not running.

The Skaarj guarding them climbed out and talked to the one driving, using a strange hissing and clicking language that reminded Haute of a snake. Haute didn't hate snakes as much as he hated Skaarj.

After a short time, the driver got out also and began work on the front of the transport. Clearly, from what little Haute understood of what powered transports, they were having engine trouble.

The other Skaarj remained guarding them, standing beside the transport, alternately staring at them and watching what the driver was doing.

Haute just stared at the guard and the red aura that seemed to radiate from around him. Haute had asked a number of Nali over the last few months about the red aura around the Skaarj. Only two of them said they had seen it, too. But that meant it was real. Very real.

The next hour slowly wore on. Haute was extremely thankful that the transport had stalled in the forest instead of in an open area. They would have cooked in the metal body if it had been out in the sun during the hours around noon. Also, without the transport running, his headache had leveled to a constant pain in his neck and head. He could stand that much, as if he had a choice otherwise.

About twenty minutes after they had stalled, Rentahs groaned and stirred.

"He's coming around," Ablee said, leaning forward and studying the young fighter.

"Too bad," Haute said. "He would have been better off sleeping through what's coming."

Ablee nodded. "That he would have." Then, as if Haute's statement had sunk in, he looked directly into Haute's eyes. "You know something?"

Haute laughed at the seriousness of his old friend. "I've seen a few things."

Rentahs moaned again and then pushed himself up on his elbows, focusing his eyes on Haute. "Where—" He stopped speaking when he saw the Skaarj guard standing beside the transport.

Haute patted the young warrior's arm. "We won the battle, but it seems that six of us have been taken out of the war."

Rentahs looked directly into Haute's eyes, and for the first time Haute could see fear in the young Nali. Complete and total fear.

It tore at Haute's heart. There was nothing he could say to Rentahs. He was either going to die, or be a prisoner in a mine. There was nothing good about either alternative, and nothing that Haute could say would make it any better.

"What have you seen?" Ablee asked, forcing Haute to look away from the fear in Rentahs' face.

Haute glanced first at Ablee, then at the others in the transport, including Rentahs. Maybe there *was* something he could say that would give them all hope.

"I've had a few visions of the future," Haute said slowly, expecting them to look at him with puzzled looks.

They didn't. They simply leaned forward, waiting for him to go on. None of them had questions about the word *visions*. Nothing. They just waited for him to speak.

Haute glanced at Ablee. "They know about my visions?"

"You warned an entire castle before the Skaarj

crash," Ablee said, smiling at his friend. "You've led us through victory after victory. It would be hard for them *not* to know."

"What have you seen?" Rentahs asked, his voice barely covering the fear that showed through his eyes. He clearly needed something, anything, that Haute could give him to hold onto.

Haute took a deep breath. "I've seen the Skaarj defeated in the near future. They will all be killed."

With that, Haute stared at the Skaarj guard standing next to the transport, putting all the hate and force he could muster into the look.

The Skaarj shifted and stepped toward the front of the transport, his red aura bending and swirling around him, as if Haute's stare was forcing him to move.

Haute was surprised at the Skaarj's reaction, then laughed at his own thoughts. He turned back to face Ablee. A look of hope was covering his friend's face. Doubt, yet hope.

"We defeat them?" Rentahs asked, pushing himself up into a sitting position and leaning against the side of the transport, clearly still very weak from his injury. "You've seen that in a vision, just like you saw them crashing?"

"I have," Haute said to Rentahs. "We will drive the Skaarj from our castles and then go on to build new and wondrous homes." Haute didn't tell them he saw those homes floating in the sky. There was no point in confusing them right now.

Ablee stared Haute, his gaze intent. "There is more, isn't there?"

Haute smiled at his friend. There was no point in telling Ablee about his coming death, either. That would serve no purpose. He would see it soon enough.

But Ablee could clearly tell that Haute was hiding something.

"There is," Haute said, his voice sad. "In the far distant future, far beyond all of our deaths, the Skaarj will return from the stars once again."

"And we will defeat them again," Rentahs said, his youthful promise holding onto the fact that Haute had told them they would win once.

"I'm afraid we won't," Haute said. "They will control the planet. Where there are only a few hundred Skaarj now, there will be thousands then. And they will be far more advanced than these Skaarj are now. We will not be able to hold them back."

"So we fight for nothing," Rentahs said, lowering his head.

"No," Haute said. "We fight to win this first occupation. During the second time the Skaarj come, the *Nali* won't be able to stand against them." He really stressed the word *Nali*. "But we will have some help then."

"Help?" Ablee asked.

Haute nodded, letting the memory of that very special vision flood back into his mind.

"There will be a beautiful angel who will descend from the heavens. She will be crippled, but she will also have the ability to shoot fire from her hands. She will come, and then the Skaarj will be driven for a second time from the homes of the Nali."

The five Mountain Fighters sitting in the back of the transport stared at him, as if soaking in his every word.

Ablee looked at Haute with a very strange expression on his face. "An angel from the sky who can shoot fire with her hands?"

Haute nodded. "I have told you what I have seen."

Suddenly, the engine of the transport came to life, and the Skaarj guard climbed back aboard and took his position.

A moment later, they were again bumping and jarring their way down the road under the noon sun, getting closer and closer to Haute's death.

Chapter 20

Second Occupation

Zofia clung to the rungs on the side of the water pipe with both hands while she took a breather. This had to be the biggest ladder she had ever climbed. It was one of two six-foot-diameter pipes: an intake and a return line for the power plant's cooling tower, though she didn't know which was which. It didn't matter anyway; both had access ladders along their full length. She'd already pulled herself up at least two hundred feet of the one on the left, and there was easily that much more to go. At least, they weren't inside the pipe. She didn't think she could have handled that.

Fortunately, with the camouflage suits, she and Gerick and Melnori didn't have to worry about concealing their approach. They had still gotten soaked; Quoin had been fired on, the moment he approached closer than a mile from the mesa, so he had backed away and dropped them off near the river, and they had floated down to the water pipes.

That had still seemed the best route to infiltrate the city. All the roads and footpaths were no doubt heavily guarded, but Melnori suspected only one or two Skaarj would be guarding the pipes—if anybody was at all.

Zofia hoped they were hard of hearing. She was panting like a Saint Bernard in the sun, and Gerick and Melnori weren't doing much better. It was hot and sweaty inside the full-body suit, especially under the face mask, which wasn't vented well enough for heavy exertion. Zofia was tempted to pull hers up so she could at least breathe fresh air while she climbed, but if the Skaarj could see infrared light she would look like a glowing Cheshire cat to anyone watching.

Rrajigar was calm at the moment. The warplane flying patrol around the city kept the resistance air force at bay. They had tried a coordinated attack, a dozen flyers going after the warplane at once, while another dozen flew straight for the city, but the warplane had outmaneuvered them so easily it was pathetic. Only one had made it close enough to drop a bomb, and none had damaged the warplane.

But now, another flash of light in the sky toward the mountains caught Zofia's attention. She looked out to see what it was—instinctively clutching the handhold at the sight of the mesa dropping away beneath her feet—and saw five or six quick stabs of light, each one ending in a bright explosion. It took nearly ten seconds for the sound to reach her; by then, the target had returned fire, but its shots didn't hit anything.

It had to be Quoin. The landing craft was the only thing on the planet that was faster than a warplane; he was harassing the Skaarj pilot, playing with him while he tested out the modifications he had made in his armament.

"Don't get cocky," she muttered.

"What'd I do now?" Gerick asked. He was right below her on the ladder, though not visible at all.

"Not you. Quoin. See him out there?"

"I was too busy panting." A pause. "Yeah, now I do. Good, take the son of a—"

His words were lost in a loud, rushing roar from overhead. A dark shape eclipsed the stars as it swept toward the two fighting airships.

"Another warplane!" Zofia said, when it had passed. "Get the hell out of there, Quoin!"

He obviously saw the oncoming plane. But he couldn't resist firing one last shot at the first plane, this time with a missile of some sort, before he lit the fusion drive and roared upward on a spear of light that lit the ground like day for miles around. The first warplane exploded in a ball of flame, burning pieces dropping to the ground to set more fires there, but even as the first plane fell, the second one fired a missile that arched out and up toward Quoin, closing the distance in seconds.

"Look out!" Zofia shouted.

"Shhh!" Gerick hissed.

The missile met the lander with just a tiny flash. There was a moment in which it looked like it might have been deflected, but then the lander erupted into a fireball too bright to look at. The missile had been tipped with tarydium.

The concussion nearly shook Zofia off the access ladder. "Damn it," she said when she could hear again. "You stupid, arrogant, reckless—*bird.*"

"He took out one warplane," Melnori said.

"Fat lot of good that did him. Or *us*. There's still one out there, so we're still completely on our own."

"Then we'd better get going," Gerick said.

"Yeah, yeah." He was right. There was nothing they could do about Quoin.

A bright spotlight shone down the side of the mesa. It slid along the pipe, right past the three invisible climbers, then winked out.

"They heard you," Gerick whispered.

As long as they don't shoot at sounds, Zofia thought, but she shut up and climbed.

They had to pause for breathers more and more often as they neared the top, but at last they were about ten feet from the spot where the pipes entered the upper pump house. The ladder went up the side of the building, and at the top of it a nervous Skaarj patrolled back and forth, looking down over the railing every few seconds. He could apparently hear their footfalls, but every time he shone his spotlight down at them he saw only an empty ladder.

Zofia paused again. She felt Gerick's hand on her ankle, but he didn't say anything to her this time, and she didn't speak, either. Slowly, carefully, she drew the camouflaged laser pistol she had gotten from the S–38 and aimed at the railing. She steadied her hand against the ladder, waiting for the Skaarj to lean back out.

He had apparently decided he was worrying about nothing. What a time for him to give up! She slapped the railing, and he popped his head back out, but this time instead of the spotlight he was pointing a stunner—one of the directed-force weapons—straight at her.

Armor wouldn't be any good against that. If he fired, it would knock all three of them off the ladder. Zofia sighted on the dark silhouette of his head against the stars, held her breath, and squeezed the trigger.

Bright green light lanced up at him and played across his head, scattering off his scaly green skin. Green! Shit, that was as bad as a mirror to a green laser!

His eyes, at least, weren't green. He roared in agony as the laser blinded him, and he fired his stunner as he fell back. The beam swept across Zofia, shoving her down, and she felt her hand slip off the rung, but Gerick shoved her hard on the butt, and she caught it again before she could fall.

"Go!" he hissed. "Get him before he raises the alarm!"

It was too late. He bellowed something in the harsh alien language, and spotlights from higher up in the city swept around to bathe the entire pump house. Nobody fired, though. They could see only a single Skaarj staggering around on the flat rooftop.

Zofia climbed up and over the railing. She heard Gerick and Melnori right behind her. The Skaarj heard them too, and he fired his stunner toward the noise, but Zofia dived to the side and rolled back to her feet again, then tiptoed to the other end of the roof.

She bumped into another invisible body, stepped to the side, and looked over the edge. Only ten feet or so to the ground, with a ladder bolted to the wall.

All three of them tried it at once. Zofia backed off, then realized the other two had done so, too, so she went ahead again and clonked heads with Gerick. She heard him swallow whatever angry word he had almost shouted at her, but she took the moment to start down the ladder, moving quickly before he could step on her fingers.

She waited until she heard two sets of footsteps

crunch on the gravelly ground, then whispered, "Let's get out of here before they figure out what's going on."

"Yes, let's do," whispered Melnori. "Follow me." He led the way toward the city proper, Zofia holding her hand on his back, and Gerick holding his hand on hers.

The resistance flyers had done quite a bit of damage before the warplane had chased them away. Zofia and her companions had to climb over piles of rubble, much of it full of sharp-edged fragments of rock. Rrajigar had been a Nali city before the occupation, and they had liked to build with stone and timbers. Zofia was glad for the armor; without it, she would have sliced her ankles to shreds in the dark.

They eventually came to an access road and followed it from the power plant to the town. They could see four tall towers reaching up into the sky, and dozens of squat buildings at their bases. Skaarj soldiers rushed back and forth, fighting the fires the first attack wave had started.

"There," Melnori said. "That tower on the right is the command center." If he was pointing, it did no good.

It didn't matter. One of the towers looked like a lighthouse, its entire top floor all windows lit from within. That had to be the one he meant. That was also the tower that the monitor on the S–38 had said housed three more human prisoners.

"We might be able to double our manpower here," Zofia said. Provided the Skaarj had left them in any shape to help out. That one file tagged "deceased" wasn't encouraging.

She led the way toward the base of the tower, fighting to remain calm as she approached three Skaarj coming toward them. A cloud of smoke wafted through, stinging her eyes, but she held her breath so she wouldn't cough.

Behind her, she heard Gerick whisper, "Shit! Get out of the smoke!"

"Why?"

"Just do it!"

She turned around, and there were the hollow images of Melnori and Gerick, patches of clarity in the whiteness like reverse ghosts. The camouflage suits collected light on one side of the body and transmitted it again on the other; that normally provided complete invisibility, but they couldn't work in a situation where light couldn't make it through.

The smoke cloud was too big to dodge. The three invaders ran for the side of a low stone building, but the Skaarj spotted them before they could reach cover. Plasma bolts crackled out through the smoke, striking Zofia and Melnori in their sides and slamming them against the wall. Zofia felt something break in the medical kit she wore at her hip, but the armor had deflected most of the blow; whatever had broken, she didn't need it yet.

Gerick fired his laser at the Skaarj, momentarily blinding them with the bright green flash scattering in the cloud, then he drew his flak gun and fired at their heads. Two of them went down, but the third got in another shot, blasting him backward. He dropped his fragger, but Zofia caught it in the air, spun it around, and fired at the remaining Skaarj. Her first shot merely blew his right arm off, but she corrected her aim and pulped his head with her second.

"We've got to get out of here," she said. "This place is going to get really busy in a few seconds."

Their armor had shielded them from the plasma

bolts, but the camouflage coating had been seared off in footwide patches. Now, three blackened splotches of soot bobbed away into the city, ducking into doorways and behind parked flyers, as Skaarj and Kraal soldiers ran toward the sound of fighting.

Zofia had hoped the guards around the base of the tower might have joined the others, but there were still five of them standing in front of the big wooden doors of the main entrance.

"Is there a back door?" Zofia whispered to the dark patch she thought was Melnori. They had snuck up to within thirty feet or so, but there was no cover any closer.

"There are two doors, but they're both the same size," he replied.

"Then let's just take this one and get it over with. Ready?"

"Ready," said Gerick. He raised his flak gun. Zofia had put away her camouflaged laser in favor of the tarydium gun; even though it didn't disappear when she grasped it like the laser had, there was no sense worrying about being spotted now, and it was a much more powerful weapon. Melnori had a plasma gun from Quoin's armory.

"Fire," said Zofia. All three weapons spoke at once. Two of the Skaarj went down immediately from plasma burns and exploding projectiles; a third flashed with light from the tarydium crystal, then when Gerick fired again, he exploded with a wet blast that knocked the last two off their feet. Zofia fired at the one on the left and missed, but the tarydium bullet ricocheted off the ground and exploded in midair right over his body, doing the same job a direct hit would have.

Both Gerick and Melnori shot the last one, but not before he had fired back at them. He wasn't using a plasma gun, but Gerick shouted, "Ow, dammit!" and something clanked to the ground in front of him. A dark line about three inches long and a quarter-inch wide had appeared on his chest where the camouflage armor had been damaged. Zofia bent down and picked up the projectile that had done it: a circular saw blade about the size of her hand. Its teeth were half an inch long and as sharp as scalpels.

"Razorjack," Melnori said. "The Skaarj love them because they can chop up their victims a body part at a time."

"Without that armor, Gerick would be missing his heart about now. Assuming he had one to begin with," Zofia said.

"Ha, very funny."

She flipped the sawblade away. "Nasty little bugger," she said. "Come on, let's go before somebody comes to investigate."

They ran past the dead bodies and pushed open the massive wooden doors. Three Kraal waited inside, but they couldn't tell who was entering so they didn't shoot immediately. They didn't get the chance; Melnori zapped one, and he fell smoking to the floor. The other two were only partly visible on the spiral stairway that ran up the center of the tower. One was above and one below; Zofia fired her tarydium gun at the lower one and saw the flash of light that meant she had hit him, but he dropped out of sight before Gerick could detonate him. He fired at the upper one instead, blowing off a leg. The Kraal fell down the stairs, growling like a mad dog, but Melnori silenced him with his plasma gun.

She heard a wail from below, then a tremendous explosion rocked the tower. Pieces of stone staircase shot upward and rattled down around her. The Kraal had finally exploded.

She went to the stairway and looked down. There was a free drop for fifteen feet or so. She had planned to go downward first, thinking that the prisoners would probably be there, but that wouldn't work now. She didn't even know if they had lived through the blast. Stupid move. Maybe criminally stupid. The only saving grace at the moment was that she didn't have time to dwell on it.

"Put that damned gun away," Gerick told her. "You'll bring the whole tower down on us with it."

He was right. She traded it for a flak gun.

The sound of many running feet came from above. That didn't seem like a great way to go, either, but there wasn't any other choice.

"Let's go now," Zofia said, "before they get organized." She ran up the stairs, taking them two at a time, and got two flights up before she met the defenders coming down. She waited until she could see the second one's head before firing at him, figuring Gerick could see the first one by that point. Their two guns spoke simultaneously—the report was deafening in the stone stairway—and the two Skaarj soldiers tumbled down the stairs, nearly knocking them down before they could dodge out of the way.

There were more right behind them. All three attackers fired at once; the flak guns rattling the stairs with their concussion, and the plasma gun sizzling and scorching Skaarj and stone both.

Razorjack blades came whirling down the stairs, ringing and striking sparks off the walls. One hit Zofia on her left arm. Her armor immediately stiffened and the blade glanced off, but the impact spun her sideways.

"This way," she said, running up another few steps to the next floor and jumping out of the stairwell.

Two dark smudges joined her in the hallway just as half a dozen Skaarj and Kraal fighters rushed down the stairs, firing their weapons. If they saw the humans and the Nali, they must have thought they were merely blast scars on the walls.

"Okay, up again," Zofia said as soon as they were gone. She climbed one more flight, then ducked aside again when she realized they were just one floor short of the top. She was standing on a circular landing around the spiral stairway, with a short hallway leading to a closed wooden door behind her. There was no evidence of anyone on this level, but by the sounds, there were at least a dozen Skaarj up above.

They had wanted to take the control center intact if they could, so they could use it later themselves to replace the destroyed resistance headquarters. Now, faced with the reality of it, that didn't seem likely.

The door behind her popped open, and a Skaarj stepped out with a plasma pistol in hand. Zofia and Gerick both whirled around and fired, but he saw the guns floating in the air and took a wild shot, then ducked back before they could hit him. The loud *boom* drew more attention from above, too. Razorjack blades and plasma bolts came down the stairwell, clanging and zapping the invaders' body armor. They fired back, forcing the defenders away from the stairwell, but the ones who had passed them going down now returned and shot upward at them, as well.

They were trapped. "In there," Zofia said, pointing her gun into the room where the single Skaarj was. It looked like an office; at least there was a heavy desk sitting at an angle under a big window. Whatever it was, if they could get in there, they would have only one doorway to defend.

The trouble was, the Skaarj was already in that position, and he wasn't offering himself as a target again. In fact, he kept sticking the barrel of his plasma gun around the jamb and firing blind, forcing the three in the stairwell to take cover.

"We've got to kill that bastard first," Zofia said, firing back to make *him* take cover again.

"That's Karrikta," Melnori said, shooting down the stairwell while Gerick fired upward. "He's the leader."

"He is?" That changed the picture. It was obvious they weren't going to surprise anybody else, but if they could take the leader, the others might surrender.

But how could they do that? He wouldn't come out to face three enemies at once. It was hard to think with the boom and sizzle of weapons' fire all around her, but at this point, everyone was just making noise. This Karrikta didn't know that, though; from where he was, he could just hear a lot of fighting going on. What if he thought the coast was clear? Or better yet, what if he thought it *wasn't* safe where he was, anymore?

Zofia reached in through the side slit in her armor and unzipped her medkit. She fished around inside it—careful of the broken glass—until she found the handball she had carried there since the crash landing.

"Okay," she whispered. "Next time someone shoots at us, scream like we've all been hit."

"Why?" asked Gerick.

"Never mind that, just do it."

They didn't have to wait long. The Skaarj in the

office shouted something in his language, and the others all fired at once. The stairwell filled with flying death. Without their armor, they would have been killed instantly; even with it, Zofia wasn't sure that Gerick's and Melnori's screams weren't genuine.

She added her own panicked yell to theirs, then cried out in Vrenic, "I'm hit! It's no use. I'm going to have to use the bomb."

Then she aimed for the angled end of the desk and threw the handball into the office. It bounced off the desk, hit the wall behind it, and disappeared into the room. Zofia could hear a couple of more bounces, one accompanied by a crash as it hit something fragile, then she saw it bounce across the floor and out of sight again.

Chapter 21

First Occupation

The castle Esiob loomed ahead as the transport bumped and jarred over the rough road, slowly edging closer and closer to what Haute knew would be his last hour.

From Jeeie's scouting reports, Esiob had been used as a sort of central headquarters for the Skaarj. And the mine there had more Nali prisoners working it than any other mine.

Haute's tarydium sensitivity was already getting bad. His headache pounded at the back of his skull like a prisoner wanting to get out. He knew that the minute they entered the castle, the pain would become so bad that most likely he would black out. He was going to do his best not to let that happen. If he was going to die, he at least wanted to be aware when it happened. A matter of pride, if nothing else.

"Looks like we're going right to the top," Ablee shouted over the consistent roar of the transport engine. Then he coughed, doing his best to clear his throat. Ablee wouldn't live long inside the castle, either, since his tarydium sensitivity resulted in his throat closing up.

The transport left the forest and entered the large open area around the front of the castle. The sun beat down on them, blinding Haute for a moment. Then he saw what was ahead and let out a gasp.

Filling the meadow, guarded by at least forty Skaarj around the outside edges, were Nali prisoners. Obviously they had been herded out of the mine and down into the open area in front of the castle for a reason.

Leaning against the castle wall was a large post.

The reason was to watch them die.

The vision of his death flooded back into Haute's mind. That post, the crowd of Nali watching. He had very little time left. Very little, indeed.

Suddenly, for the first time, he was deep down afraid.

Ever since the first vision and the marathon trip to warn his family, he had managed to hold his fear inside, trapping it in a little place deep under layers of action and hatred. Little flashes of the fear had escaped at times during the fighting, but he had always managed to hold it down, keep it contained and under complete control.

But now, seeing the vision of his death taking shape, the fear broke loose. His hands were suddenly shaking, his stomach felt like a knot, and the blackness of passing out threatened to swarm in from the edges of his headache and take him down.

He forced himself to take long, deep breaths, blowing out as hard as he could.

Ablee touched his shoulder. "Tarydium?"

Haute didn't even dare answer him. He didn't

believe he could control his own voice, let alone anything else.

The transport jerked to a halt, and the engine shut off, letting in the sounds of the Nali crowding the field. Murmuring sounds.

Whispering.

Some crying.

The headache pounded at Haute as he fought his fear.

The Skaarj guard roughly shoved Ablee, Rentahs, and the other three Mountain Fighters out of the transport, letting them move into the crowd of Nali.

Haute watched as Ablee stopped, turned, and stared at him, his mouth open, worry filling his face.

Haute took another deep breath. He had to remain calm. He couldn't let the fear take him.

Not now.

Not when so many were watching him.

For them, and for the future of the fight against the Skaarj, he had to be strong.

The lump of fear that had spread through him suddenly vanished, as if it were nothing more than a layer of dirt he had washed off. He took one long breath and let it out, then smiled at Ablee.

Around him, the crowd stirred at his smile.

They were all watching him.

He let his gaze move out over them, smiling, doing his best to look confident, not let the fear show.

The Skaarj guard grabbed him roughly by the arm, the monster's claws digging into his flesh. He dragged Haute from the transport and toward the pole leaning against the stone wall near the front archway of the castle.

Instead of letting the fear back in, Haute focused all his anger and hatred at the Skaarj who was dragging him, not giving him the dignity of walking under his own power.

The red aura around the Skaarj seemed to waver and flicker, like a flame in a wind.

The Skaarj tripped and then stopped.

Haute stood and stepped forward, almost ahead of the guard.

The guard increased the pressure of his grip and continued slowly, almost as if climbing a steep hill. Haute walked beside the guard, his head held high, his gaze moving over those in the crowd. He tried to remain looking as calm as he could, for them. And for himself.

But inside, his mind was racing. Could it be possible that his thoughts could affect the Skaarj? That didn't seem likely. Or possible. But on the other hand, it had just happened. He had seen it.

Then he realized that the visions may have been nothing more than his thoughts. His visions had warned his people and helped defeat the Skaarj at four different castles so far. His visions, his thoughts, had fought back.

The Skaarj guard shoved Haute down at the base of the pole. Then quickly, two other Skaarj picked him up, while a third tied his body to the post with vines.

Vines covered with thorns.

The pain filled his body, his mind, every inch of his being.

His vision had warned him of the pain, but now it seemed worse, more intense, as the thorns jabbed into his skin, cutting him in hundreds of places.

He bit down hard on his lip, not allowing himself to cry out, not allowing himself to let the fear flood back in.

In the crowd, Haute saw Ablee start forward.

Rentahs grabbed him and held him, not letting him move forward to be killed for nothing.

As they tied him to the pole, Haute looked directly into his old friend's eyes and shook his head no.

For a moment Ablee continued to struggle against Rentahs' grip, then stopped.

Blood dripped down Haute's arms and legs from the hundred cuts from the vine's thorns. But there were so many cuts that none of them really stood out. Only the pain in his head dominated the agony he was going through.

Three Skaarj roughly picked up the pole and moved it forward, dropping it down into a hole dug in the ground. Suddenly he found himself upright, held that way by the vines and thorns, staring out over the crowd of Nali.

They were completely silent, their faces set in looks of shock. Tears ran down some faces. Others were taking silent, shuddering breaths.

All for him.

While one Skaarj piled brush in a wide circle around his feet, the other two moved up to him and began poking at his arms and legs. At first, he couldn't figure out what they were doing, exactly. But as they worked, the pain increased in each cut.

And in his head.

Then one of them moved around in front of him, and he saw what they carried: small slivers of pure tarydium.

They were stuffing tarydium into his cuts, under his skin.

The pain seemed to grow throughout his body as more and more of the slivers were shoved into his wounds. He could have never imagined such pain.

Again he bit down on his lip, not allowing himself to scream or even whimper in pain as he fought the blackness that wanted to pull him away. He wouldn't let it. He needed to remain here, see the end of his vision and his own death.

The headache seemed to grow from the back of his head like an ugly black wave. They shoved more and more slivers of tarydium into his cuts.

He fought against the blackness, concentrating on the faces in front of him.

He would not pass out. He would not.

Finally, the two Skaarj finished and stepped back, making clicking sounds that Haute took to be almost laughing.

Ablee watched, holding Haute's gaze, giving him strength. Haute took the strength from his old friend and used it to push back the pain, numb the arms and legs, shove the threatening blackness away.

A Skaarj stepped forward through the archway gate and stopped in front of Haute, facing the crowd of Nali. He seemed to be taller than the others, and Haute, even through the intense pain, could tell that he was the Skaarj who was in charge.

Beside him, another Skaarj held up a small box. Something Haute had never seen before.

The Skaarj spoke in clicks and grunts, but from the small box a Nali voice came out, hollow and empty, echoing over the silent crowd.

"You will watch the one you call prophet and leader die. You will understand that fighting the Skaarj will only bring you death."

Haute, through the pain in his mind, didn't completely understand the words of the Skaarj. The only thing he completely understood was that he was being killed as an example. An example that might stop the fight of all the Nali. Haute couldn't allow that to happen.

The Skaarj leader turned and nodded to one of the guards.

Haute focused on the leader, glaring with all his might, all his hate, all his pain, at the one who had ordered his death.

A Skaarj guard stepped up and started the brush around his feet on fire.

The red aura around the Skaarj leader seemed to flicker as Haute focused and focused on it.

Haute could see Ablee glance at the leader of the Skaarj, then back at Haute, then back at the leader.

For an instant of time, it seemed as if nothing would happen. Then the leader staggered back and almost fell as the red aura around him flickered.

Haute's mind realized that he had actually affected the Skaarj with his thoughts, somehow, some way.

"Focus your hate on him!" Haute shouted to Ablee.

The fire around him was slowly gaining in intensity. The slivers of tarydium were burning in his skin. In a very short moment they would ignite, burning him far sooner than the fire itself.

Burning him from the inside out.

He looked away from the leader of the Skaarj out on the masses of Nali. Then, taking a deep breath of the smoke, he shouted again, "Focus your hatred on the leader."

Ablee instantly understood.

"Trust me one more time!" Haute shouted to all the Nali watching. "Focus your hatred on the leader."

Then Haute turned his head and stared at the leader, his gaze burning into the leader's eyes, his thoughts those of destruction.

He focused all his hate.

And then he took the energy from the pain of all the slivers of tarydium under his skin and focused it at the hated monster.

Focus.

Focus.

Ablee and others in the crowd had turned and were doing the same thing.

The red aura around the Skaarj leader flickered quickly.

The pain of the burning tarydium under his skin threatened to black Haute out, but he fought on, focusing the pain through his eyes at the Skaarj leader.

The large monster staggered, and the Nali gasped.

Then, as a unit, they focused on the Skaarj.

The slivers of tarydium in Haute's legs burst, flooding intense pain through his body as the flames licked up his legs.

The Skaarj leader spun like a drunk, staggering, as the others around him worked to help him.

Then, just at the moment that Haute felt he could no longer hold on, the Skaarj leader burst into flame.

A bright blue flame that seemed to eat the leader's red aura like a fire devouring dry grass. It swallowed the Skaarj leader and jumped to those trying to help him.

Then, as Haute realized, deep inside, that again he had beaten the Skaarj, the rest of the tarydium under his skin exploded into flame.

He had won.

And he had lost.

Yes and no.

The voice from the cave echoed through his mind as the pain filled him and he passed into the blackness of death.

Chapter 22

Second Occupation

Karrikta had chosen the worst possible moment to use the waste sucker. It had seemed like a good opportunity at the time. The aerial bombardment had ended with the arrival of the warplane, and even though the pilot had stupidly allowed himself to be shot down by the only serious resistance threat in the air, a second warplane had taken that pilot out and continued to fly patrol around Rrajigar. None of the outer perimeter guards had reported trouble since the one to the southwest had ceased communicating, and the ones closer in had seen no action all night.

It was beginning to look like the resistance had spent itself in one aerial attack. Karrikta had decided to take a moment to take care of a pressing urge, but he had just hooked up the apparatus in his office wetroom when he heard the commotion at the base of the tower. You don't interrupt a waste sucker in mid-job; Karrikta had stood there, frustrated and panicking while the pumps strained against his involuntarily tightening muscles and he listened to the battle advance up the stairwell.

He had pulled free the moment he could and rushed out to see what was going on, only to find three alien weapons floating in the air before him. He had shot his close-quarters impaler at them and jumped back just as they had fired at him, but in his haste he had missed, and they fired again if he showed so much as a gun barrel around the doorjamb.

There had been dark patches in the air, below and beside the weapons. He recalled the mental image of what he had seen and decided it had to have been someone in stone-colored camouflage that had been scorched in places.

So they could withstand single hits. Maybe he hadn't missed.

He took a deep breath and bellowed loud enough to be heard throughout the tower, "All at once, fire into the stairwell!" He stuck his impaler around the corner and pulled the trigger again and again, and he heard shots from above and below, as well. It sounded like a full-scale war in the echoing stone structure.

He heard screams of agony, too. Good. When the shooting had died down, he heard someone say, "I'm hit! It's no use. I'm going to have to use the bomb." And a projectile flew into his office, glanced off his desk, hit the wall beside it, flew across the room to ricochet off the wall beside the door and knock a priceless crystal hologram off a shelf before careening toward the trophy heads on the far wall.

He was glad he had just used the waste sucker; otherwise, the sudden pressure as all his muscles spasmed in shock would have led to embarrassment. As it was, he had to fight for coordination enough to scramble out of the office. He looked back just as the bomb hit the button under Berggren's head and activated his last words.

"Beware of . . . pretense," the warrior's voice said to the empty room. "I nearly defeated you . . . with misdirection."

"No!" he screamed, firing his impaler at the floating weapons before him. Its plasma beam crackled outward, but a flash and a roar struck back. He felt a sharp tug on his gun hand, and searing pain shot up his arm. He looked down and saw a bloody stump where his wrist used to be.

"Surrender or die," said a disembodied voice. It didn't sound like a Nali. Was someone else making a grab for the planet? Someone with better technology than the Skaarj, apparently. The attackers' camouflage was good; aside from the burned spots, it was completely invisible.

"Never!" shouted Karrikta. He lunged toward the voice, swiped his remaining hand through the air, and hit something soft. It hardened the moment he hit it, though, and his claws merely glanced off.

One of the alien guns blasted him in the chest, knocking him backward and ripping his skin away down to the ribs. He hit the door frame and fell into his office, rolled to the side, and slammed the door closed, but three more blasts shredded it and sent splinters into his wounds. The barely visible attackers kicked it in and rushed into the office.

He couldn't get to his feet without his arms to help him balance. The desk tipped over toward him; all his papers and pens and data storage equipment crashed to the floor; then the desk thumped down on his legs, pinning him in place.

"We've got your leader!" the voice shouted.

"Throw down your weapons, or we'll take him apart piece by piece."

"Don't do it!" he shouted. "There're only—" Something landed on his mouth and shoved hard. A foot! He howled and swiped at it, but even when he batted it aside, it came right back.

"He's already lost an arm. You've got to the count of three before he loses his other one. One . . . two . . . three."

Nothing happened. "Tough luck," said the voice. The weapon shifted toward his good arm. He lurched to the side just as it fired and it blew a hole in the floor, but that only bought him a moment. The invisible gunman fired again, and his shoulder erupted in agony. He screamed, then clenched his teeth over the sound. When he tried to move his arms, nothing happened.

"Three more seconds and he loses a leg. One . . . two . . ."

He heard a clatter of weapons in the stairwell.

"No!" he yelled, or tried to, but the foot kept the sound from escaping his mouth.

"You've got more than that," said the voice. "Come on, toss all of 'em, or he'll be considerably shorter than he is now. Gerick, throw his arm up there to show 'em we mean business."

There was a wet thud, then a shower of weapons fell into the stairwell. There weren't many guns in the control room; those fools were actually disarming themselves. Coin counters and technicians; all the true warriors were outside manning the defense guns.

His chest and what was left of his arms hurt worse than any pain he had ever felt before. His arteries had constricted to reduce his blood loss, but whatever they had shot him with didn't kill the nerve endings; those were all transmitting signals at peak capacity right out to the bloody ends of his stumps. It was hard to concentrate through the constant agony.

He couldn't fight the pain, but he could use it. He let it drive him into a killing rage, thrashing back and forth and biting at the foot in his mouth. He managed to shake the desk up and down, but he couldn't get out from under it; each time he flexed his legs enough to push it upward it fell back on him even harder than before.

He howled an inarticulate—and muffled—roar of frustration. "I think he's losing it," the voice of his torturer said. "Should we put him out of his misery?"

For the first time since the attack, icy fear swept through him. He hadn't really considered until now the possibility that he might die. He had always won his battles, even the one against Berggren, who had been the five-to-one favorite in the betting pool. Karrikta had been given his position on Na Pali long after the true fighting was over, and what few battles he had fought since then had been so one-sided they were laughable.

Now the truth was inescapable: he had grown soft.

Another voice, this one a Nali, said, "Don't kill him unless we have to. He's worth more to us alive than dead."

Saved by a Nali. The humiliation alone should have killed him, but he ashamedly admitted that he didn't care where salvation came from so long as he didn't die.

A small part of him, the last vestige of rationality, pointed out that if he died now he would go down in history as the person who had lost the biggest tarydium reserve in the galaxy, but if he lived, there was still a chance he could redeem himself.

He clung to that thought even when he heard the *boom, boom, boom* of heavy weapons' fire and the screams of his underlings being slaughtered in the command center and on the stairs below. Of course, the attackers had killed all of them as soon as they were disarmed; that's what Karrikta would have done in their place.

He heard startled cries from the Nali, and more fighting in the command center, when the soldiers on the roof descended to see what the commotion was, but his hope died along with the soldiers. Then the whip came off the wall from beneath his Nali trophy and bound his legs together. The desk rose off his legs, and he felt invisible hands grab his feet and drag him out into the stairwell.

"I can walk," he told his captors when he realized they intended to drag him backward up the stairs. He could see their outlines now; their armor was blackened in many places.

"That's the problem," said the leader's voice. He still couldn't place it. "If you can walk, you can also run. We'll try not to bang your head up too bad, but we need you upstairs, and we're not untying your feet. And after seeing the way you bite, I'm not getting close to your head, either."

He would have hated to see what they would have done to him if they weren't being careful. As it was, there was much cursing and tugging and bumping of his head, and he nearly passed out from the pain, but they crawled their way upward a step at a time until he was stretched out on the command center floor.

The mysterious invader shoved a microphone into

his face. "Here," said the voice. "Issue the order to surrender."

He looked at the tiny plastic pickup hovering in front of his face. That was the battle commander's microphone. Karrikta couldn't see the transmitter setting, so he had no idea who it was broadcasting to, but if these invaders truly expected him to order his troops to surrender, then it must be set to wide dispersal.

This wasn't quite the chance to redeem himself that he had been hoping for, but it would have to do. At least, anyone who survived would know he had given his life to defend his charge and his honor. He thought over his words carefully, knowing he would get only a few, then shouted in the Skaarj language, "Attack the command tower! Aliens have overpowered us!"

The microphone was snatched away. "What did he say?" the voice asked.

The Nali translated his words into Vrenic.

"That ought to do the trick. Gerick, are you ready up there?"

"Ready," came the faint voice of someone on the roof.

"Here it comes."

The soft growl of the warplane that had been patrolling the city now changed pitch. With growing horror, Karrikta heard the click of switches being snapped and the quiet warble of the transmitter being returned, then the Nali said, "Attention resistance units. Commence full assault. Target rooftop defenders on all buildings *except* the command center. Repeat, command center has been secured."

Karrikta lashed out with his feet, kicking at anything within reach. "You tricked me again!" he yelled. "Who *are* you?"

210

"The avenging angel," said the voice.

A chill spread through him at the words. He had heard that phrase before, from the Nali whose head he had hung in his office. "The avenging angel will bury you," he had said.

"Liar!" he shouted, not sure at the moment whom he was talking to. It didn't matter; nobody responded.

The warplane drew closer, but long before it got within firing range, the antiaircraft guns on the roof fired a continuous stream of tarydium-tipped projectiles at it. The pilot hadn't expected that, not if he thought Karrikta was still able to use the radio in the room below. The plane didn't have a chance; the sky lit up with the explosion, and pieces of metal rained down on the city.

"The warplane is gone," the Nali said to the resistance troops.

Some of the antiaircraft gun crews on other rooftops had no doubt seen that the shots that destroyed it had come from within the city, but either they hadn't seen which tower they came from or they couldn't bring themselves to fire on the command center. After a moment, it didn't matter anyway; they were busy fighting off an entire sky full of Nali flyers. Karrikta could see only a tiny fraction of the battle from his vantage on the floor, but what he could see and hear was enough. There were way too many aircraft to knock down, and each one that got through took out a rooftop gun. Some of them also landed and disgorged troops, who set to work on the soldiers in the streets. The entire city sounded like the inside of the command tower had not long ago, right down to the dying screams of the Skaarj defenders.

"Who *are* you?" Karrikta asked again of the shadowy figure who hovered near his head. He tried to prop himself up on his right arm, forgetting that most of it was missing, but the intense stabbing pain reminded him that he was just a torso with legs now.

"I told you," said the voice.

"You told me nothing," he replied. "You're not Nali; I can tell that by your manner. I may die of these wounds, but before I do I have the right to know who killed me."

"You've got the right to a swift kick in the teeth," said the voice. "But I'm feeling generous. Here." He heard motion, and a patch of pinkish skin appeared in the air. It grew larger as the invisible layer was drawn upward and back, until he was looking at a Hhuman face. The flickering light from weapons' fire and the screams of the wounded lent it a sinister air that the ones in the prison cell below had never possessed, but the face was Hhuman.

"I knew it," he whispered.

"Then why'd you ask?"

"To be certain," he replied. His wounds were more serious than he had thought; he had to gather his strength before speaking again. "Who sent you?"

The creature rubbed its chin. "That's a damned good question. But I guess when it comes right down to it, I sent myself."

"You'll never succeed in driving the Skaarj from Na Pali. We'll find your homeworld and enslave you. We'll *eat* you."

"Big talk, from someone who's tied up on the floor."

"I ate one of your kind yesterday."

"I ate one of yours just an hour or so ago. He gave me gas."

The other Hhuman—for Karrikta was sure that's who the second non-Nali had to be—called down from the rooftop, "Melnori, stop the air strikes! I don't think there's anyone left alive to bomb."

The Nali relayed that information to the attacking forces, and slowly the sky cleared. Karrikta lay back on the floor and listened to the last of the fighting on the ground, but that didn't last much longer. Rrajigar was lost.

Chapter 23

First Occupation

Haute, the Nali his people called Prophet, stood in the entrance to the cave high on the mountain. Behind him, he knew the voice's crashed spaceship was crammed down into a mass of metal, a hulk that had been dead for years. In front of him, a beautiful sunrise was spreading pink and orange and purple colors over the sky, announcing the birth of a new day. The mountains and valleys below him were dark, the sun not yet pushing the night away. A cool wind brushed him, feeling heavenly against his skin.

He glanced at his arms. No wounds from the thorns on the vines. No burns from the flames and the tarydium. What had happened?

The memory of the pain of dying on the pole, with tarydium slivers burning under his skin, echoed through his mind as he tried to grasp what he was doing here. One instant the fire was taking him, the next instant he was standing in the cave of the crashed spaceship, watching the sunrise.

"How is this possible?" Haute said. "Voice? Guide me!?"

Your questions are imprecise.

Haute wanted to laugh, but the memory of dying was still too close, too real.

"Did I die on that pole in front of the castle Esiob?"

Your life ended there. Will end there. Is ending there.

"Then how do I stand here?" Haute asked after a moment of letting the knowledge that he really had died sink in.

I am not confined by the limits of time. You stood there. Therefore you stand there.

Suddenly Haute understood. Just as the voice had helped him see the future, he could also visit the past. Like a memory, only far more real. Just as his visions of the future had been real. He was only limited by the power of his mind.

"Voice," Haute asked, "would it be possible for you to show me what occurred after the moment of my death in front of the castle?"

The cave vanished.

The castle lay in front of him. He had no body, but instead seemed to simply float near the tops of the forest, behind the crowd of Nali.

A body, his body, was tied to a pole near the castle archway, burning. Yellow and blue smoke drifted upward from the fire, floating on the wind through the blueness of the afternoon sky. His face had already turned black, and he could see that his skin was melting off. For some reason, the sight of his own burning body didn't bother him. He felt as if it should, but it just didn't.

A number of Skaarj bodies were also on fire, burning, it seemed, from the inside out. Flames were shooting from their eyes, the mouths, their stomachs.

So he hadn't imagined that the Skaarj leader had burst into flame. He thought he might have, in all the pain.

He had actually been able to destroy a Skaarj by simply focusing on him. He had no idea how it worked. Possibly something to do with his sensitivity to tarydium.

He clearly wasn't the only one who had the power to kill with thought. Ablee and others in the crowd below were turning their attention to the Skaarj guards. As a number of them stared at a guard, the guard staggered, tried to run, then burst into flame.

With each burning Skaarj, Haute wanted to cheer, to urge his friends on with the battle.

They didn't need his cheering. They were doing just fine on their own.

Ablee continued to lead those focusing on the Skaarj, burning one after another, while Rentahs and a few others scrambled to grab the rifles of dead Skaarj.

Quickly, the scene became one of mass fear as most of the Nali prisoners bolted to get away from the fighting. But dozens and dozens stayed, fighting with their minds or with rifles until there were no more Skaarj left in front of the castle.

Then they started inside.

Haute knew the outcome, now. He didn't need to watch any more.

"Thank you, voice," Haute said.

Instantly, Haute found himself sitting in one of the huge chairs in the wondrous triangle-shaped room on the voice's spaceship. Stars were flashing past the two huge windows into the universe, showing that the ship was moving at a very fast speed.

Haute leaned back, content in the fact that his

death had led to the final defeat of the Skaarj. It made it feel all worthwhile, for some reason.

For the next hour, Haute just sat there, letting the stars flash past, thinking about his family, his friends, his people. Nice thoughts. Warm thoughts. The only sadness was the fact that he would miss them a great deal. And he would miss seeing his nephew and niece grow up.

Then it dawned on him that he just might not. He was limiting himself again. At the moment, he was sitting in a dead spaceship. And he was dead, or had died at one point in time. But as the voice had been trying to explain to him, there were many points in time. He stirred and sat up straight. The room, as usual, was empty, except for himself.

And the voice.

The voice that had been his guide and friend now for some time. A friend that was still with him, just as Ablee was with him always during the years they were together.

"Where are we going?" Haute asked aloud, his voice filling the large room.

Your question is imprecise.

"Okay," Haute said, laughing. "Where and *when* are we going?"

Better. Much better. Where would you like to go? I am only a guide.

"And a very good one, too," Haute said.

The voice didn't respond, it seemed, to compliments.

"I would like to go to two places," Haute said. "First, I would like to visit my brother and his family ten years after the time I died. See how they are doing."

Second?

"I'd like to go into the future and watch the angel from the heavens fight the Skaarj. See how she does it. On second thought, let's go there first."

Around Haute, the triangle room vanished, and he found himself floating above an open field, in the far distant future, staring up at the sky as a spaceship hurtled toward the ground. A spaceship with an angel from the heavens on board.

Chapter 24

Second Occupation

In a cellar below the ground floor, the three prisoners were still alive. When Zofia heard them calling through the thick wooden door, she felt a great weight drop away from her. In all the fighting she had done, after all the Skaarj and Kraal she had killed, it was the fear that she might have inadvertently killed three of her own kind that weighed most heavily on her conscience.

"Hold on," she called through the door. "I'll get you out of there." She examined the lock, saw that it required a key even from the outside, and said, "Stand back. I'm going to blast it open."

"Just a second," came the reply. There were scraping sounds, then, "All right."

She aimed her flak gun at the massive cylinder and pulled the trigger. The *boom* shook the walls, but the explosive bullet did the job; the door swung open to reveal two young men and an older one rising up from behind a thick mattress. They still wore their blue prison uniforms, but they looked clean and well fed.

"Boy, are we glad to see you," said one of them. The only reason they *could* see her was because the camouflage suit had finally given out. The city was theirs, but the Skaarj weren't all dead or captured yet; even without camouflage, Zofia planned to live in her armor until they were. Gerick and Melnori were still out helping round up the last of them, but after she had thrown Karrikta into a prison cell, she had come to rescue the other humans.

"Glad to see you, too," she said. She looked into the cell, saw how small it was and that there was only the one mattress, and said, "Looks like it must have been pretty cozy in here."

The younger two blushed. The older one snorted.

"What?" asked Zofia.

"The Skaarj bastard who captured us wanted us to breed," he said.

"Oh," said Zofia. "That must have been before— what was her name, Sandy?—before she died."

"Sandy was a man, too," said one of the kids. "And a pretty smart one, to boot. His quick thinking kept us alive. When the Skaarj said he wanted more humans, Sandy promised him we'd deliver."

Zofia narrowed her eyes. "But . . . how did Karrikta think . . . ?"

The older man coughed. "He didn't know, and we didn't think it would be smart to tell him. Sandy just told him we needed privacy and comfort and lots of time."

"But . . . what about sex? Didn't he make sure you . . . ? I mean, anything to stay alive, but the odds of all four of you being gay are kind of slim, aren't they?"

The kids were still blushing, but they laughed, and one of them said, "Doesn't matter. Wanna have sex with me, now?" He held out his hand.

Zofia backed away. "Look, kid, I know you're glad to see me and all, but—"

"Here," he said. He took her hand before she could retreat out of reach, shook it vigorously, then let go and said, "There, we've just had sex. As far as the Skaarj know, at least."

Zofia felt herself blush now. "You're kidding. He actually thought that's all there is to it?"

The older man said, "Who knows what he thought? At first, he was all hot for us to breed, and then he started going on about a conspiracy to take over the planet. Tried to get us to confess that we were behind it. We didn't know anything about it, but it looks like maybe you do."

"It's a long story," Zofia told them. "Come on, we can use all the help we can get mopping up."

She helped them climb the knotted rope up onto the ground floor, where Melnori waited. He was wearing the same expression she had seen on his face in the cavern after the Skaarj attack.

"What's the matter?" she asked.

"We have the situation under control," he said. "Except—except for Ranel. She insisted on leading the aerial invasion. She was killed even before we stormed the tower." He looked away. All four of his arms hung slack at his sides.

"I'm sorry," Zofia said. She reached out and put her arms around him. "I'm sorry," she said again.

"What do we do?" Melnori asked.

She looked up at him, surprised. "Do? You take over where she left off and finish what she started." When he didn't reply, she said, "You, Melnori."

"No," he said. "I could never do that."

Zofia looked at the three liberated humans beside her, who were eyeing Melnori's four arms, then looked back at the Nali. She admired his peaceful nature, but it was a definite liability at times. "What do you mean? You don't have a choice. You're the next in command."

"No, I'm not," he said. "You are. You're the avenging angel. Everyone agrees."

She laughed. "Cut the crap. You just made that up to shame me into helping you, and you know it."

He jerked free of her arms as if she had bit him. "What? I did no such thing. It's the prophecy, made centuries ago! An avenging angel will come down out of the skies to help us defeat the Skaarj."

"Sure," said Zofia, "and I've got a nice little asteroid around Jupiter I can sell you, too."

The men laughed, but Melnori shook his head and said, "Do you think Karrikta was part of this deception? Remember how he reacted when you told him who you were? Why would he call you a liar if there was no prophecy?"

He had a point, Zofia supposed. So Melnori had used an existing legend to coax her into helping him. But the notion that she could be the person some religious nut had prophesied hundreds of years ago was ridiculous. She was a prisoner, maybe even rightfully so. Everything she'd done since coming to Na Pali had been done out of either desperation or selfish calculation. If she was the Nali avatar, then they were in bad trouble, indeed.

"There is nobody else but you," said Melnori. "Whether or not you believe you are the angel, we do, and that's what matters. You must lead us now, or all we have accomplished will come to nothing."

"Somebody has to, that much is true," she said. The Skaarj in the other cities wouldn't wait for the Nali to reorganize before they struck back. Someone had to put together a coordinated defense force to hold Rrajigar, and at the same time make plans to advance on the next stronghold before the Skaarj could bring in reinforcements from off planet. "But I still don't see why it has to be me."

"Who, then?" asked Melnori. "I am unfit for the job. Should we ask Gerick?"

Zofia shuddered, though she wondered if she was being unfair. She hadn't forgotten who had first joined her call to arms in the cave when the Nali had seemed ready to give up. Under that rough exterior lived a person who was, if not compassionate, at least honorable in his own way.

But was he a leader? Not one she'd want to follow.

She looked back at the three other ex-prisoners. Two young kids, probably street punks who'd gotten in trouble with the law or crossed somebody more powerful than they, and an older man of unknown potential. Maybe he'd be a good leader, but nobody would follow him until he had proved himself.

She reluctantly came to the realization that Melnori was right: of all the candidates for the job, she was best qualified. The Nali should have been scared out of their minds at that prospect, but they apparently thought she was some kind of divine manifestation. What a crock—except Zofia could still feel that little tug of doubt. What if it were true?

She was still wondering the same thing a few hours later. She had Karrikta's massive desk tipped upright and had set herself up in his old office, where she was starting to get a picture of the forces at her disposal. She was making a list of resources and liabilities as she learned about them. Two hundred and twelve air vehicles had survived the attack on Rrajigar, and there were maybe thirty more Skaarj flyers from the city that could be pressed into service. Soldiers numbered anywhere from five to a planetful, depending on whether or not she counted the Nali as "soldiers." Weapons weren't a problem; they had captured more today than the entire resistance had owned beforehand.

The Skaarj, on the other hand, still had six warplanes, about a thousand troops, three major cities, and dozens of mines and outposts scattered all over the planet. They also presumably had a functioning spaceship or two, plus the cargo ships that carried refined tarydium to their homeworld.

It was a pretty lopsided list. The only thing that made it even faintly balanced was their one ace in the hole, if they could get it to fly again: the camouflaged S–38 that still waited out in the badlands. It was designed to fight the Skaarj, and it was far more deadly than Quoin's modified landing craft had been. Its original crew would never have lost it if they hadn't been using it for espionage instead of in a straightforward battle.

Of course, there was a downside to the S–38, as well. Inuit Corporation hadn't built it out of the kindness of their hearts; they wanted Na Pali just as badly as the Skaarj, and they had undoubtedly built more than just one S–38. They probably wouldn't move against the Nali as long as the Nali were doing their fighting for them, but the moment the war was over, there would be an even bigger one to follow.

She penned that in a separate column and entitled it, "Worry About Later." She could fight only one war at a time.

She wondered why she was worrying about it, at all. By the time Inuit entered the picture, she could repair the S–38 or capture a Skaarj ship and be long gone. That had been her intent since the crash landing; why change course now?

She tried out the possible answers like ill-fitting shirts.

Because she liked it here? Ha. She'd been shot at and on the run ever since she'd arrived.

Because she was afraid to go back to human space? Certain parts of it, maybe, but there were lots of colonies where she would be safe and might even be able to live a fairly normal life if she kept her nose clean.

Because she wanted to avenge Boris's death? She still felt his loss like a bullet through her own heart, but her blood lust had died sometime after the third or fourth Skaarj she had blasted to pieces.

Maybe she was staying because she liked to feel needed, for a change. Or maybe it was all of the above. When it came right down to it, she did like the planet, at least the parts of it she'd seen. She didn't really care if she saw another human world anytime soon. Her memory of Boris would always be a motivating factor in whatever she did. And on top of all that, no matter how much she protested, it was gratifying to feel needed, whether she was fulfilling some kind of mystical prophecy or just providing a perspective the Nali couldn't bring to the situation themselves.

She looked back at her list of resources. There was one other thing to put in the plus column, though Zofia gave it about as much credence as the prophecy of an avenging angel. Melnori had told her about a legend that the first wave of Skaarj had been defeated centuries ago by some kind of psychic weapon that used their own tarydium-based body chemistry against them. If that was true, Zofia wanted to know why they didn't use it again, but Melnori had merely shaken his head sadly and said, "Prophets with psychic powers are apparently even rarer than avenging angels."

Apparently so, but that was one more thing she would have to look into when she got the chance.

Zofia set her pen on the desktop and contemplated the heads on the wall. Gruesome things. She would have to take them down once the dust had settled.

Or not. Maybe she would be better off putting up one of her own. Karrikta's, perhaps, when he was no longer useful. Keeping heads on the wall would add to her mystique, and it looked like mystique was her strong suit with these people.

Around and around it goes, she thought. What if they were right? What if she really *was* some kind of alien avatar? The notion was ridiculous, but a good commander had to cover all the angles.

So she considered the possibility for a moment, savoring the thought. What if she was? It wouldn't affect the Nali; they already thought so. It wouldn't affect the humans, because nobody would believe it. It wouldn't affect the Skaarj, because they would have to fight back, no matter what. When it came right down to it, the only person it really made any difference to was Zofia, and the mere fact that she was considering it was more important than whether or not it was true. Just entertaining the possibility that it *might* be true meant she had somehow, somewhere, acquired the self-confidence to believe that such a thing might be possible, and that told her more than any revelation from the heavens could.

Hard Crash

The Zofia who had been sentenced to death a month ago had indeed died. Before coming to Na Pali she would never have imagined herself leading anything, but now she was no longer content to be a pawn in somebody else's game. Pawn, hell; she wouldn't even be the queen. She would be the player. She would be the game itself. She would invent a *new* game if that's what it took to realize her potential. Avenging angel, hah! She was Zofia Mozelle, human being. What others thought was their own problem.

Chapter 25

Second Occupation

On his way upstairs to the command center after locking up the last of the Skaarj to survive the invasion, Melnori looked in on Zofia and found her asleep with her head on the desk. Karrikta's personal trinkets—and quite a bit of his blood—still covered the floor, but Zofia's mere presence in the room made it unquestionably hers.

He studied her face, so alien and yet so expressive. He was learning to read her emotions; right now, she looked pensive, even in sleep. Her eyes twitched beneath their lids, and a victorious grin momentarily twisted her features. She looked almost demonic when she did that. Capable of anything. She had been wearing her camouflage hood over her face when she had blasted Karrikta's arms off, but Melnori would be willing to bet that was the expression she had been wearing at the time.

He reached down to his belt and touched the plasma gun he carried there. He knew what he must look like when he fired a gun. Totally panicked, leavened with equal parts revulsion and self-hatred. That he had fired one as often—and as well—as he had tonight was a testament to how far he had fallen. That the fall was necessary was no excuse. His psyche had been scarred forever by the experience.

And what of Zofia's? He had watched her carefully over these last few days, and he didn't think she was the same person she had been, either.

For one thing, she was the avenging angel. There could be no doubt now. He had been playing with her at first, leading her on and trying to shame her into helping his cause, but somewhere along the line she had become the very thing he had mocked her with.

This had been just the first battle in a much bigger war, but Melnori felt strangely calm as he contemplated the battles to come. He knew, with an absolute faith that defied all logic, that Zofia would guide the Nali through them all, until the Skaarj were just a fading memory.

But what then? Melnori watched his sleeping salvation, and wondered. There was no prophecy to cover what came after. The avenging angel would defeat the Skaarj, but beyond that, the Prophet had been silent. Perhaps that was because the outcome was so obvious. Any fool could see what the lure of a planet full of tarydium did to people. Could Zofia—a mortal being, no matter what else she was—resist that lure?

It would be interesting to see. But if not . . .

Melnori silently drew his plasma gun and sighted down its barrel at her head. He fought down the urge to gag, fought the urge to drop the gun and run screaming into the night. He held it there, pointed steadily at her head until he came to grips with the idea that he could take her life if he had to. For the sake of his own people.

He holstered his weapon and turned away to let her rest, but he stopped when he saw the faint orange line through the window behind her. It was the first hint of dawn breaking on the eastern horizon. They had worked the night through, and the sun was rising on a new day.